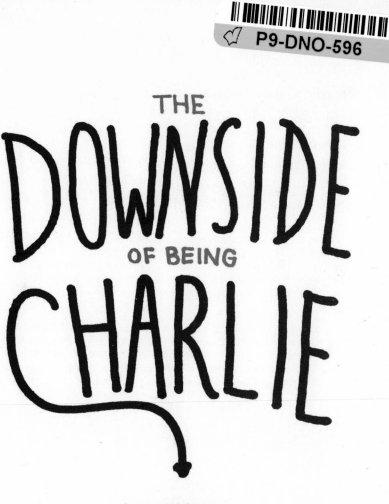

THE DOWNSIDE OF BEING CHARLIE

by JENNY TORRES SANCHEZ

To my sister Nancy, for being there when I needed you most.

ISBN 978-0-7624-4401-4

Library of Congress Control Number: 2011933870

E-book ISBN 978-0-7624-4532-5

9   8   7   6   5   4   3   2   1
Digit on the right indicates the number of this printing

Cover and interior design by Ryan Hayes

Edited by Marlo Scrimizzi

Typography: Century Schoolbook, Futura, and Eurostile

Published by Running Press Teens
An Imprint of Running Press Book Publishers
A Member of the Perseus Books Group
2300 Chestnut Street
Philadelphia, PA 19103–4371

Visit us on the web!
www.runningpress.com

THE DOWNSIDE OF BEING CHARLIE

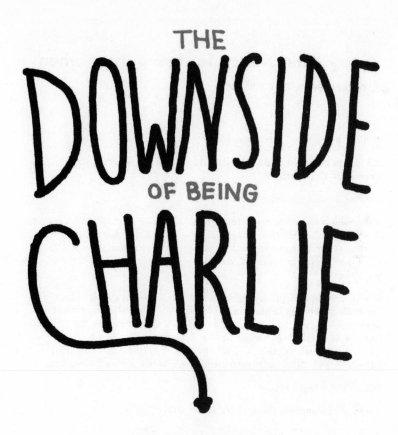

by JENNY TORRES SANCHEZ

RP | TEENS
PHILADELPHIA · LONDON

PART ONE
ZOOM IN

CHAPTER ONE

I don't know how you can see something before it's actually there, but you can. I guess it's the signs, right? Like little pieces of a gigantic invisible puzzle, all coming together, but you don't see what you're supposed to see, don't know what there is to know, until they're all attached and you step back to look at it. And then you think, I should have known. But the thing is, you already did.

Here's when I knew but didn't really know:

When she hadn't come to the phone the last couple of times I had called home.

When Dad picked me up from fat camp all by himself.

When he acted like he always did when she was gone, like nothing was wrong, when in fact, everything was wrong.

When we both avoided bringing her up the whole car ride home.

And then I came home and saw what I already knew. Mom had left us . . . again.

•••

The day before the first day of school, I'm hanging out at my best friend Ahmed's house, anticipating what the year will be like.

"You're money, baby!" Ahmed tells me as he stands staring into his closet dressed in his blue velvet smoking jacket. Ahmed has been my best friend since the fifth grade, and yeah, he actually owns a smoking jacket. I laughed my ass off the first time I saw him in it. I thought I was looking at a pimp or something, but now it seems totally normal. It's totally Ahmed.

We're in his room when he says he thinks I might actually have a chance with a girl this year. I swivel around in his chair, staring at the Rat Pack posters on his walls for the millionth time. Ahmed is obsessed with the Rat Pack. There are posters and postcards of them all over his Las Vegas–themed bedroom, and there's actually a really funny one where Ahmed went to all the trouble of taking a picture of his face, cropping it to size, and pasting it on the poster so he looks like he's crooning into one of those old-timey microphones with the rest of them. He's the only guy I know that has pictures of old men in suits up on his walls. Anyway, Ahmed tries to be smooth and cool like those cats but he's not. He's gangly and completely ADHD, always bouncing around or fidgeting, which must be why he's so damn skinny, like his metabolism is on turbo speed.

"Trust me, baby, this is going to be your year," he says.

"Yeah, doubt it," I tell him, although I hope he's right.

"No, I'm serious. I mean, okay, so I know you were hacked when your parents sent you to Camp Fit but . . ."

"Fat camp. Just call it fat camp, like it really is,"
I say.

He was right. I was pissed that my parents shipped
me off like that. Actually, it was more so my dad, after
he and Mom had a big fight in the beginning of the
summer. I should've known at dinner that night, when
I reached for my third helping of meat loaf and mashed
potatoes, or when I followed that with two helpings of
chocolate ice cream, courtesy of Mom who always kept
the freezer stocked (when she was around). Dad didn't
say anything as I stuffed my face, but I could feel the
way he kept looking at me, and then how he kept looking over at Mom. And later as I hid in my room, I
couldn't help but press my ear up against the wall to
get a better listen to Mom and Dad's muffled voices on
the other side of the wall.

It had been awhile since we'd all sat down to eat
together, so maybe Dad forgot how much I could put
away, or maybe I forgot to hide it from him the way I
usually did, but did he have to make me sound like such
a mess? *We have to help him, Carmen. Did you see how
much he ate? My God.* His words made me cringe, and
my face and ears got hot and sweaty as I pressed them
harder against the wall. Mom insisted he was being
ridiculous and that nothing was wrong. They went back
and forth, Mom making light of everything Dad said,
which, of course, made Dad even more pissed, and the
whole argument ended with an emphatic decision for an
immediate intervention.

He actually used the word intervention. Like I was
an addict—a screwed-up food equivalent of a meth head.

I pictured myself panhandling on the streets for money to buy a box of Ho Hos, scrounging up a couple of bucks, and heading to the nearest gas station to buy the vanilla crème–filled goodness. The clerk would recognize me and shake his head as I shoved it in my face, making grunting noises like a wild boar.

Intervention.

My dad thought I needed professional help. I'd never felt like such a fuckup in my life.

So when he came in my room the next day and proposed I go to fat camp, giving me some bullshit spiel about starting off my senior year on the right foot, along with a bunch of other motivational crap, there were two things I could have done instead of just shrugging my shoulders and saying, "sure." I could have told him the last thing I wanted to do was go to Fatties Anonymous where I would talk about my excess corpulence and see my gross self reflected back at me through all the other fat losers there. Or I could have sided with Mom—but I've learned to never side with Mom, which basically means there was only one option.

See, siding with someone usually means I have your back and you have mine. It usually means you might be wrong but we'll pretend you're right because there are two of us and majority rules. But siding with Mom doesn't mean that. Siding with Mom means siding with the current mood or state of mind that she's in, and Mom's moods and state of mind change at lightning speed (which means that whoever thinks for one delusional moment that she might have their back is dead wrong). The one who thinks they are on the same team with Mom is left totally fucked when she prances on over to the other side or leaves the field altogether.

"Okay, fat camp," Ahmed says, "but *look at you*. You look good, my man! Might even get a little hey-hey with that chickie that moved in down the street." Ahmed says this in his usual Rat Pack lingo. Sometimes it makes him sound like a dumbass, but he doesn't seem to care, even when people look at him funny. I think Ahmed has convinced himself that in all his Rat Pack glory, he transcends even the coolest teenager. I don't give any indication that what he's said means much to me, though he has just voiced what has become my secret mission this year: getting Charlotte VanderKleaton to notice me (in a good way).

The first time I saw Charlotte VanderKleaton was a week before I left for fat camp. I was walking to Ahmed's to tell him about Dad's messed-up plan when I saw her and her family moving into the McGoverns' old house. She was sitting on the front porch swing, holding a flowerpot with reddish-orange flowers the same color as her hair. She was just sitting there swinging, and I swear it looked like she was talking to these flowers, petting their little petals. She was the most amazing girl I'd ever seen. I don't usually believe in all that crap about auras, but I swear, she kind of glowed.

Okay, it *had* been an unusually hot day for early summer in North Carolina, and with all that extra weight on me, some could argue that I was simply overheated and hallucinating, but I know I saw somewhat of a glow surrounding Charlotte. I came to a dead stop, my mouth hanging wide open. When she looked over at me on the other side of the street and waved, I could've died because I could only imagine what I looked like in all my sweaty, fleshy wonder. I stared at the cement, pretending not to see her, and continued to Ahmed's. But secretly, in the darkest recesses of my mind, in those places we have embarrassing thoughts that we're glad no one else has access to, I made a decision. I thought, if Dad is going to make me go, I'll lose this weight *for just a chance with this girl*. I'll come back a brand new person, someone who could actually talk to someone like her. So I didn't wave back because I didn't want her to remember this guy ever again.

I never thought girls like her actually existed. She's not like other pretty girls that guys jack off to in the secrecy of their beds at night. She's different. She doesn't walk; it's more like she floats. And every time I've seen her, something always sparkles, her skin or her hair or her lips (God . . . her lips). I thought it was bullshit that people met someone and instantly fell in love with them. But that's how I felt about her.

"Although . . . ," Ahmed breaks into my thoughts, "she and Mark have been cozying up this summer quite a bit. I don't get how that fink got to her so fast. He doesn't even live around here."

Ahmed wasn't telling me anything I didn't already know. I'd seen Mark Delancey's car over there enough since fat camp to know something was going on. And I wondered how Kennedy High's notorious prankster and all-around glorified jerk had managed to weasel himself into her good graces.

"Whatever. It's not like it matters. Like Charlotte

would ever give me the time of day anyway," I tell Ahmed, leaving out my plan to him, so when it doesn't work out, I don't have to feel like such an ass. I try to play it cool. But now Ahmed's got me thinking about Mark, and I start to wonder just how close those two have gotten. The thought of Charlotte with another guy, especially someone like Mark, makes me feel like someone is squeezing my lungs.

"Listen, Charlie, if you're gonna get with the ladies this year, you gotta act like you're the shit—know what I mean? Be smooth, toss a little smile her way, say hello, and when she smiles back, act like you don't care. What happens then, you ask? Well, then you got the little chickie just aching for you, wondering if you're gonna look her way again. Know why? Girls like drama. They want to yak and cluck with the rest of the hens about whether you looked at her or talked to her or brushed up against her in the hall. They don't want guys who are there no matter what. The last thing you wanna do is let them know you're into them. If they know that, it's all over. Then, they thrust their heels right into your stupid little heart and stomp all over you. Trust me. I know." He taps his foot on the floor and smacks his hand against his thigh incessantly.

Ahmed is heavy on relationship advice now because he dated Tina Capelli for exactly three months and two days last year. Tina was Ahmed's first real girlfriend, and he'd fallen hard for her. I thought it was pretty interesting that he was telling me how to be such an ass when he had totally gone all gaga over Tina—bought her flowers for no reason, opened the door for her, walked her to every class even though he ended up getting a ton of detentions from being constantly late to his classes. He even dropped me for a while because he was spending so much time with her. He'd gone the whole nine yards, but it wasn't enough. They broke up right before summer because Tina was going to Jersey for the entire vacation. She told Ahmed she couldn't have fun, real fun, if she had to worry about a boyfriend back home. Basically, it was her way of telling him she was going to be hooking up with other guys left and right all summer long. Nice. Ahmed was devastated. He even cried. But we made a pact never to talk about that again—and I mean he wrote an actual pact and made me sign it. *Ahmed's Rat Pack Pact*, he called it, and he outlined a creed of appropriate Rat Pack behavior, one of which was never cry for a chickie—and if that should happen— never, never, never discuss the incident.

It's not like I don't appreciate the advice Ahmed gives me. God knows I could use it if I really wanted to get with Charlotte. What former fat boy couldn't? I should be taking notes. I should be scribbling away like he's freakin' Hugh Hefner. But sitting here talking about her, thinking about Mark, knowing tomorrow is the first day of school and the last day to set my plans to get Charlotte VanderKleaton into effect, I feel sick.

The truth is, I hadn't come up with an *actual* plan. Even though I'd lost some weight (though I could still stand to lose a good twenty pounds more) and I'd gotten a few new items in my wardrobe, I still didn't have the smooth skills to actually talk to this girl. And talking to her would probably be a prerequisite to getting with her.

What was I thinking? I'm suddenly glad I never told Ahmed about how Charlotte was my motivation for losing weight. I'm glad he doesn't know that as I jiggled my fat ass in a frenzy of jumping jacks and sprints, I was thinking of her. And now, I really didn't want to hear Ahmed talk about girls and how cruel and heartless they can be.

"Tina back from Jersey?" I ask. I know it's a low blow, but I put it out there anyway. After Tina, all Ahmed did was go on these long, random tangents about girls and, ironically, the best way to stop it was to mention Tina.

Ahmed stops twitching and straightens up.

"Don't know. Don't care. I don't talk to that dame anymore. She couldn't handle the sophisticated stylings of a man like myself. In fact, my man, I have no idea what I ever saw in her anyway." He pulls up the collar of his smoking jacket. I don't bother to tell him that, in fact, we both know exactly what Ahmed saw in Tina Capelli since it was impossible to miss the two swelling mountains on her chest that every boy in school wanted to conquer.

"Hey, how do you know that new girl's name anyway?" he asks, his mind backtracking to something I said five minutes ago, which is usually the case with Ahmed. He abandons his search for the perfect button-down shirt and skinny tie that will let all the ladies know he's back on the market and throws himself on his bed, props his feet on to the wall, and proceeds with an improvised tap dance.

"Heard her mom calling for her," I tell him, which is true. I'd actually started jogging around the neighborhood when I got back from fat camp with the pretense that I had to stay in shape and lose more weight, but really, for the more important purpose of getting another look at Charlotte. And it was on one of these jogs that I passed her house and heard her mom calling her from the car to help bring in the groceries. Charlotte. Beautiful, amazing, intoxicating Charlotte. And I thought maybe it meant something that her name is Charlotte and mine is Charlie—both beginning with "Char"—and then I got lost in the thought that we were destined to be together.

"Aha, so you got the nerve to do a little stalking did you? Get a little peekaboo in her window, too?" He grins.

"Shut up." I get up from the swivel chair at his desk. The idea of peeking into Charlotte's window makes me feel ashamed and excited at the same time.

"I gotta jet," I tell him. "My dad will be home soon, and I told him I'd take care of dinner tonight."

"All right, Betty Crocker. Pick you up tomorrow. Be ready, my man, it's our senior year! Senior year! Woot!" Ahmed jumps off the bed and does some crotch-grabbing Michael Jackson moves. "Watch out, ladies, here I come!" he yells in a high-pitched voice.

"See you later, Freak," I say as he moonwalks across his room.

I walk home thinking of what tomorrow will be like. I hope Charlotte is in some of my classes. I wonder if she will remember the fatty on the sidewalk that didn't wave back to her that day and figure out it was me. When I think of that day, I'm secretly grateful Dad did this, even though at the time I could've decked him for insisting I was going to enjoy it.

I mean, sure, it was true that once I got there it was kind of nice not being the only fat kid around. For once, there were others *much* bigger than me, and I didn't look completely out of place. But the truth is, I couldn't stand being surrounded by those rejects. They were all so pathetic and weak. And since I didn't want to make any new friends, I sure as hell couldn't partake in the black market of Ring Dings and chocolate bars that ran through the place like a freakin' drug cartel, so I had to suffer all summer long with no one to talk to. But screw them. I chomped on my lettuce, did the exercises, and the weight actually started coming off, and then I thought, *wait . . . I can do this*. And I did.

I should've been ecstatic when the last day of camp finally came and Dad drove up in his black SUV and threw my suitcase in the back. I should have been grinning from ear to ear that I'd lost thirty pounds of fat that had apparently put me in the category of immediate intervention. I should have been pissing myself that my pants were falling off, that I'd shown Dad I wasn't as pathetic as he thought, and that I had actually learned some stuff and was determined to go home and continue this shit on my own. I should've been dancing because I would never have to see these freaks again. But I wasn't, because despite this momentous and felicitous occasion, as I got in Dad's car and listened to his congrats and what I think looked like a glimmer of pride in his eyes, I already knew. Mom was gone.

Maybe she left because Dad made me go to fat camp. Maybe she left because I didn't side with her. Maybe she left because the moon was half-full or because there was a 30 percent chance of rain. Who the hell knows. I'm tired of trying to figure it out because here's the thing: my mom is a perpetual runaway.

I know, that doesn't make sense to anybody but me, but that's what she is. She just runs away. I don't know why; I don't know where. We just wake up sometimes—and poof!—she's gone. Then we wake up—and poof!—she's back. Dad pretends not to notice or care. Mom pretends not to notice or care—or maybe she really doesn't. So I have to pretend not to notice or care. And that's just the way it is.

What we usually do when Mom leaves is pretend she didn't, but I always wonder where she is. Even though I don't want to, I come up with 101 possible scenarios. Then I have to snap back to now, remind myself that this stuff happens all the time, and I should just forget about it. And I do because it's not like I want her around. I wouldn't even care if she decided to never come back, so long as she would just tell us, so I don't have to sit here and wait, wondering why she left. Even when we're doing something, we're really waiting to see if she comes back. We take out the garbage. We watch TV. We make dinner. Dad goes to work. I hang out waiting for school to start. We wait.

CHAPTER TWO

Ahmed picks me up the next day in a full peacock blue suit and wing tips. I shake my head wondering why I was destined to have the most abnormal of everything, including my best friend. Here I thought I was pimping in some ripped-up jeans, a plain white T-shirt, and the black studded wristband that Ahmed told me to take a chance on, to *use as inspiration for a new look, a new style, a new beginning, baby!* I get in Ahmed's car (aka the Roller Skate), with Frankie (aka Frank Sinatra), blaring on the stereo (which is pretty embarrassing, but whatever).

"I see you're trying to downplay things this year," I say.

"Man, don't hate on my style. Not many people can pull off these threads. I look like the shiz-nit." I grin and nod. He's right.

I shift in my seat and think of how Ahmed certainly did not have me in mind when he set his sights on this car. If I hadn't lost the weight, there's no way I would fit inside it. It's one of those tiny, good-for-the-environment kind of cars, but to the extreme. Ahmed called me up one day last summer and said, "Smart car. FORTWO. Look it up. It's mine." I did a search for it and started laughing my ass off when I saw it.

"Dude, that car could fit in your butt crack. I thought you would get a big boat, you know, like a caddie or something."

"Nah, man. Boat cars are cool and all, but this is too AWESOME!" he yelled into the phone.

Ahmed worked like crazy the rest of that summer, all of last school year, and all of this summer at the local supermarket as a bagger. He squirreled away every cent he made (except for what he spent on flowers for Tina) and three weeks before summer ended, for his seventeenth birthday, his parents told him they'd put up the rest of the money as a birthday and early graduation gift. Ahmed almost exploded. He picked out a white one with blue stripes on the sides and named it the Roller Skate.

We zip into a parking space. I'm feeling okay as we walk up to the main school building. We turn some heads as we pick up our schedules, and while that's usually the case when I'm with Ahmed, I can't help noticing how people's eyes linger on me instead of moving right past me the way they usually do. I know it's because of the weight, which makes me feel oddly good and weird at the same time. Ahmed peers over his sunglasses at any cute girl we pass, then whistles and croons, "Hel-looooo . . ." or "Ring-a-ding-ding . . ." The younger girls smile and giggle. The older ones give him dirty looks, before looking my way. Looks of confusion and then shock cross their faces.

"Dude, this is weird," I whisper to Ahmed as one girl says a little too loudly, "Oh my God, is that *Chunks*

Grisner?" I can't tell if the way she says it is good or bad.

"Shake it off, my man. It's gonna be your year, remember? Your year."

I nod. We head over to the tables set up in the courtyard to pick up our schedules. Ahmed's right. This is going to be my year. I'd spent three years hiding in my own fat rolls, and now that I'd gotten rid of them, things were going to be awesome. I put on the cool shades that I hadn't had enough guts to wear, and do my best *I'm bored as shit waiting for my schedule but I look cool as hell* pose. When I get my schedule, I grab it from the guy with a bit of attitude before scanning the pink-and-white half sheet.

"Oh, crap," I moan, suddenly deflated of all my short-lived confidence.

"What?" Ahmed says as he studies his.

"I got drama sixth period."

"So?"

"Drama? Come on. Those kids are freaks. I didn't even sign up for drama. I can't get up in front of people and act."

"Chill, man. It'll give you a chance to strut your stuff." He grins because Ahmed can imagine nothing better than strutting his stuff.

"This sucks!" is all I can say because I've decidedly lost all desire to strut my stuff. "You think I can just get a schedule change? I can get it changed, right? Right?"

Ahmed mumbles a *yeah* as he looks over his own schedule. I fold the paper in half and make a mental note to stop by the guidance office after school. Even though administration always says they won't make any "unnecessary" schedule changes, they usually do. And this was certainly necessary. And then I try to tell myself no big deal. I refuse to let anything bring me down today.

"Let's find our lockers," Ahmed says and we head toward the 200 hall.

As soon as we enter, we see the huge crowd gathered at the end of it. We pass locker after locker, and I read off the numbers. Pretty quickly I realize that the crowd is gathered right in front of where my locker should be. We push our way through some of the kids, and soon it becomes all too obvious that the worst thing that could happen to me this year, what will guarantee that my senior year is a complete bust, what I never even thought to imagine, has happened.

"Oh, my man, total bombsville," Ahmed says, sucking his teeth. "Tough breaks, Charlie." He shakes his head.

"Crap," I whisper as I stare at what will be the bane of my senior year.

"Literally, my man, lit-er-al-ly," Ahmed says. I give him a pissed-off look. "Sorry." He says and concentrates on smoothing his tie.

I watch Tanya Bate scrape what definitely appears to be crap . . . poop . . . feces . . . waste . . . dung . . . caca . . . shit . . . out of locker 243. My locker. Actually, it was *our* locker. Out of the one thousand other seniors at Kennedy High, I was the unlucky soul randomly chosen to share a locker with Tanya Bate this year. I choke on my own spit and cough until Ahmed gives me a hard whack on the back.

Everyone in the hall gives Tanya Bate a disgusted

look as she walks over to the trash can. Rebecca Sutter smirks and taunts Tanya as she disposes of the poop, which I'm desperately hoping is just dog poop.

"What happened, Tanya? Couldn't hold it in? Sicko!" Rebecca yells.

Tanya brandishes the paper, now streaked brown, at the ever growing and widening circle around her. She laughs as they back away.

"Funny," she announces loudly, rolling her eyes at nobody in particular, but at everyone in general. "You are all so extraordinarily funny!" She shakes her head as if the prank is stupid and beneath her.

It's not like I'm Mr. Freakin' Popularity, but I still managed to find my little niche. Most of us did. I mean, we didn't all have the looks or grace or coordination of the jocks and cheerleaders, but we still fit into some category. I, for instance, fit into the "invisible fat boy who does his homework, gets good grades, hangs out with an oddball friend who has enough confidence and moxie for the both of us" category. It's not ideal, but it's served me well and helps make the whole torturous experience of high school just a little more bearable and maybe even a little fun.

Others subscribe to the school of Band Geeks, who go to band competitions together (and apparently do other things you would never think a Band Geek would do) and meet in the band room for lunch and carry their hard black instrument cases that double as protection from Band Geek haters everywhere. Or there's the Drama Kids who are loud and dress up like Smurfs for no reason other than to call attention to themselves.

They prance around the school like little imps laughing at hundreds of inside jokes and stay at school till all hours of the night rehearsing for the next performance of a lifetime. Then there are the Intellectuals, the Anime Lovers, the Preps, the Stoners, the Gamers, the Goths, the Jocks, the Cheerleader Wannabes, the Break-Dancers, the Ordinaries, the Yearbookers, the Do-Gooders, the Recycling Nazis, the Proud-to-Be Nerds, the Not-So-Proud-to-Be Nerds, etc., etc.

The point is, no matter how strange or weird or uncool you are, you fit in somewhere—unless, unless, you had the incredible misfortune of being Tanya Bate. She is nowhere near being in the same ballpark as the rest of the general high school population. Not on the field, not in the stands, not even in the same state where said ballpark exists. Tanya Bate was off on her own.

My first real glimpse of the queerness that is Tanya Bate was last year in my English III Honors class. It was a small class with plenty of desks, so, of course, Tanya sat alone. It made sense, I guess, because even in the hallways people moved away from her when she walked too close, as if mere proximity would mean catching the freak disease from which she so obviously suffered.

Each day she came in, dressed in her usual *Lord of the Rings* T-shirt and stretch pants, sat down and scowled at everyone who entered, waiting to be provoked so she could display her talents of being a real smart-ass. I never would have guessed this is what she was really like. I mean, I'd heard of her, had caught sightings of the infamous Tanya Bate before, but had never really observed her up close. Ironically, for being the most unpopular kid in school, everybody knew exactly who she was, but nobody could stand her. So I was kind of looking forward to having a class with her to see what she was all about. The first thing I noticed was how some kids—those who, like me, had never had a class with her—would come in, spot her, and stare at her with quiet intrigue as they slowly walked to an empty seat a safe distance away. I think they were scared she might bark and growl at them—which considering the stories, was not completely out of the question. Other students would groan and shake their heads as soon as they saw her. I soon learned why.

Tanya Bate is the kind of person who is aggravatingly incessant—incapable of shutting her mouth when she believes she is right, which is always. That pisses everyone off and makes them hate her more because she isn't playing the game. She isn't going by the unwritten high school rules that state if you're a geek or a freak, you have to shut the hell up unless spoken to and call as little attention to yourself as possible. But since Tanya was off on her own, I guess she didn't know the rules, or just didn't care about them. For example, at the beginning of that year, Mr. Blitz told the class that we would write our own poems in the form of "Theme for English B" by Langston Hughes.

"Can we do it in the form of a sonnet?" Tanya asked, peering at him through her thick glasses. This would become a constant question throughout the rest of the year as we all learned of Tanya's apparent obsession with Shakespeare and the English Renaissance. Everything she wrote had to be in the form of a sonnet. We all stared at Tanya and her frizzy hair that was parted down the middle, and consequently sprouted on either side of her head like two wiry puffs of teased wool.

"I'd rather you didn't. I want you to capture the same feel and tone of Hughes's poem," Mr. Blitz answered.

"So you want us to write who we perceive ourselves to be, as long as we do it like someone else, Hughes specifically?"

He looked up as if he were waiting for a thought bubble above his head to produce the answer. "Well, yes, I suppose that's right," he said after a moment.

"Isn't that kind of oxymoronic?"

"No, Miss Bate. It's actually quite simple. And I'm sure you're quite capable of understanding the meaning of the assignment," Mr. Blitz replied calmly.

"But it seems to be contradictory," she immediately countered. "Seriously, does no one else see this?" Tanya was, if nothing else, tenacious. She went beyond the point that was fun for the rest of us to watch. Whereas most classes kind of had that teacher versus students element to it, any class with Tanya usually turned into teacher and students unite to take down Tanya.

"Just do it and shut up!" yelled Kris Keller, our school track star.

"You're over thinking this, Miss Bate," Mr. Blitz called from his desk.

"But . . ."

"Shut it!" Kris yelled.

"But . . ."

"Just do it, Bate," another student called out.

"I'm just saying. How can you all NOT see this?"

Exasperated groans and sighs filled the room.

Mr. Blitz, smug and pleased, said, "The class has spoken. Just do the assignment, Miss Bate. It will be a grade."

"Fine," Tanya said, and slammed her notebook open, mumbled loud enough for everybody to know how ridiculous this assignment seemed to be, how Langston H. would just turn over in his grave if he knew the injustice that was taking place here, and what a blank, blank, mumble, mumble Mr. Blitz was to ask her to write about who she is and dictate how she write it, and some other craziness in her own secret language that nobody else really paid attention to, until at last she became completely engrossed in writing her poem. She smirked and snickered, and I swear, gave Mr. Blitz evil looks that made me wonder if Tanya practiced witchcraft.

I don't know. Tanya was a freak and all but the last ten minutes of class, when Kris went up there and read about—surprise, surprise—the glory and freedom of running and the wind blowing in your hair, and then some other girl named Terry who had tons of friends read something about the essence of her soul being lonely and bare, and so on and so forth, all I could think of was . . . *What did Tanya write?* Her poem was probably pretty damn funny, ragging on Mr. Blitz somehow, which he must have suspected. Even though her pasty arm went up each time he asked for volunteers, he just ignored her and then called on someone else, and then she would slam her hand down on the desk and roll her eyes so they looked like those freaking cuckoo owl clocks that roll back and forth, round and round. I remember sitting there in awe of her because she was a complete disaster—repelling, scary, and intriguing all at the same time. And in a weird way, she was more rebellious and antisocial than the best wannabe outcast at our school, except it didn't seem to work for her.

So, she wasn't quite what I expected. And even though I wanted to detest her like everyone else did, I didn't. To me, she was kind of funny and as I sat in class trying to be invisible, I secretly cheered Tanya on and smirked at all the ballsy stuff she said. She didn't care what anyone else thought and part of me wished I had the freedom to not give a shit like that. But I did. I remember slinking down near the back of the class, trying to sink into my own fat rolls while Tanya sat front and center for the whole world to see.

"Charlie? Yo, Charlie?" Ahmed tries to bring me out of my shock. Tanya stomps back to our locker in her brown stretch pants and *Lord of the Rings* T-shirt, and slams it shut. My mind still can't comprehend the fact that I've been assigned a locker with her. I don't necessarily think she's the most despicable person on the planet, but everyone else does and now I'll be dangerously close to being despicable by association. I, Charlie Harrison Grisner, am doomed to share a locker with Tanya Who-Everybody-Hates Bate during what's supposed to be the best year of my high school life.

• • •

I avoid my locker like it's an infection all morning. By third period, the general shock has worn off, but anger sets in as I think of my whole senior year going down the tubes. I walk into my photography class, which has a familiar smell that makes me feel slightly better. Most people think photography is a nothing class, which I guess it could be, but I've been taking it ever since freshman year and am hoping I can do it for a living since there's really nothing else I can think of doing. But not like a wedding photographer or anything like that. I'm not so keen on the idea of spending the rest of my life capturing Aunt Bea belligerent and drunk, or little Sammy doing the Macarena. It's just not me. Instead I'd like to work for National Geographic or something, where I could travel all over the world and wouldn't be stuck here.

I have photography fourth period, which is nice because it's right before lunch, and if I'm really into something, I can stay and work—but only if this new photography teacher is okay with students hanging out in his room. Some teachers are and some teachers aren't. Mr. Pratt, the photography teacher who'd been here since 1964, didn't care, but he retired at the end of last year. Mr. Pratt was cool, but only because he was old and had obviously stopped giving a damn a few years ago. You could tell he was tired of the whole high school scene. Sometimes, he just looked out at us and I'd imagine he was thinking *Holy crap . . . what a bunch of idiots*. Other times, it was like he wasn't even there. I guess when you do something long enough, you don't really have to be there anymore.

I'm the first person in class. The new teacher is tall and thin and wears a brown corduroy jacket with those little brown patches on the elbows and slightly ripped-up jeans. He looks sort of young, sort of old, and wears black-rimmed glasses that are the newest way to portray coolness and nerdiness at the same time. They say, *look at me, I'm cool, but . . . also smart.* The ripped-up jeans are such an obvious ploy at establishing that he's not one of "them"—conventional, conformist, republican, old. You know.

"Hey, there," he says as I come in, "have a seat wherever." I walk over to the seat I've sat in for the past three years.

"So, advanced photography . . . must really like it then, huh?" I nod. More kids come into the class, most of which I recognize because we've been in Photography I, II, and III together. They look at me, some acknowledging me with a confused nod, like they're wondering where the rest of me is. I nod at a few of them, and then busy myself with studying my already memorized schedule. It was the same in my other classes, with some idiots actually feeling the need to announce loudly, "Holy shit, Grisner, you look different!" I thought it would be cool, coming back and proving myself somehow, but the constant attention to my weight only made me feel more self-conscious, and by the time photography rolled around, I was over it. As if that weren't enough, everyone kept probing me on how I did it and then I had to skirt the whole fat camp business. Finally, the bell rings and the teacher introduces himself.

"Hi, everyone, I'm Mr. Killinger," which we already

know since it's printed on our class schedules. "Most of you know, Mr. Pratt has retired, which means I get to take his place, and I am truly excited about getting to know all of you and your work."

Blah, blah, blah. The standard introduction crap. Pretty soon he'll have us playing the name game. Didn't he realize this was our fourth year of photography and the class pretty much ran itself? I'm weary of the new guy and probably a bunch of "new and exciting" things he'll want to put in place. I study the rest of my schedule and try to figure out the quickest routes to each class.

"I'm sure that you all are quite serious about the art of photography." I look around wondering if anyone else is buying this. Instead I notice how most of the girls are all smiles and looking at each other like, "yes!" They'll probably be swooning over him all year.

". . . so, I'm not going to give you guys a lot of little meaningless stuff. Instead, I have loftier plans . . ." This guy must read poetry and listen to obscure music—what do they call it? Adult alternative?

". . . is the director of the fine arts department at Rennington College. He's also an amazing photographer and my mentor, which means every once in a while he'll do me a favor. Now, it took some convincing, but he's agreed to display the best collection among my high school students alongside student and faculty art at the college's annual winter exhibit." He pauses and looks around. The class is listening pretty intently, especially since he mentioned Rennington College, one of the most prestigious colleges in the area with a solid reputation for its Fine Arts department. I have to admit, he's piqued my interest, but isn't this a bit much for the first day of school? Hadn't this guy ever heard of the freaking name game? I listen, but I'm thinking this might be one of those projects teachers come up with that totally fails. You know, the kind that sounds great until you suffer through it and then plans fall through and it somehow blows up in the teacher's face, then they don't end up grading it and you realize you just did a whole bunch of crap for nothing.

"The work displayed at this exhibit is quality stuff, guys. So, you should start thinking about what you'd like to do and you better help me prove to Dr. Hoyt that high school students can produce some fantastic stuff. I know this is a lot to go over on the first day, and it's still a few months away but, well, what else is there to do, play a lame name game?" He laughs. There's a round of smiles and laughs in agreement.

"The winter exhibit is in early December, and you have to have at least five quality, well-thought-out and executed frames that are great individually, but also come together to tell a story in your collection." Mr. Killinger goes to his desk to grab a stack of papers and starts handing them out to the class. "This is something that I'm only opening up to Advanced Photography IV students, so while the odds are in your favor, the competition is stiff." He goes over all the components and requirements of the assignment. Everyone asks a thousand questions, most of which are all similar questions stated in a bunch of different ways, which are also already answered in the handout. No wonder Mr. Pratt retired. But then Rod Stevens ask the bonus question of the day—"is there a prize?"

"Actually . . . ," Mr. Killinger stops and thinks for a minute before going on, "I was going to wait and use this as incentive later, but okay," he continues, "in addition to having your work on display, Dr. Hoyt did mention something along the lines of a possible scholarship, if and only if the work is of exceptional quality."

Everyone seems excited. Mr. Killinger looks out at the class and smiles, satisfied with the reaction. He's got the whole class buzzing. He's won. He's popular. They love him. And it's annoying.

• • •

I thank my lucky stars that Ahmed has a car, even if it is the tiniest car on the planet, and people laugh and point as we drive by them. Ahmed loves the attention. I don't, but whatever, I'm just glad I don't have to ride the bus this year because according to the unwritten laws of Kennedy High, you officially reach loser status if your senior-ass hits the green vinyl of a bus seat. You're pushing your luck even as a junior.

We get in the Roller Skate, and I pull the itty-bitty weightless door shut with too much force. The car shakes like crazy. I look over at Ahmed.

"Don't worry about it, Chuckie. It's all good." He clicks on the engine, and we zip out of the parking lot, weaving through and cutting off monster cars left and right.

"So, what do you wanna do?" he asks, "Hungry?" I nod.

"Biff's?"

"Burgers? Dude . . ." I look over at Ahmed.

"Sorry, I forgot. But . . . aw, man, come on! They have sandwiches and turkey burgers, too. Can you get something like that?"

"Yeah, I guess," I tell him, already thinking of the torturously greasy aroma at Biff's.

I envy Ahmed who can order a double cheeseburger with extra cheese, large fries, a large coke, *and* apple fritters sprinkled with powdered sugar, and he still looks like a praying mantis. So looking like a praying mantis isn't every teenage boy's dream, but when you've looked like a fat green caterpillar your whole life, you envy the mantis. Being fat is brutal. The names for one—Chunks, Chunky, Chubs—almost anything but Charlie. And you just have to laugh and pretend like you're in on the joke. It's even difficult to enjoy a slice of pizza because everyone looks at you like "no wonder." It gets old after awhile.

"Turkey burger, no mayo, no cheese, on a whole wheat bun and . . . a side salad," I tell the guy behind the counter. I feel like a girl right now.

"Dressing?" he asks.

"Got low-fat?" He looks at me funny.

"Low-fat Italian," he says. I nod.

"Drink?"

"Just water . . ." I'm *totally* a girl. "Football season," I lie. He looks at me and shrugs.

We scan the place and spot an empty booth. Ahmed unwraps his dripping cheeseburger and takes a huge bite of it. The ketchup and mayonnaise squirt out of the bun and drip down his chin. My mouth waters as I open the wrapper of my burger. It looks nowhere near as juicy or delicious as Ahmed's. I take a chomp out of it, chew, and wash it down with water.

We're talking about our different classes, when Tanya Bate walks in with her mother. She looks just like Tanya, but with long frizzy gray hair instead of brown. They both wear the same thick glasses. The only difference between the two is that Tanya's mom apparently doesn't have an obsession with Gandalf or Bilbo Baggins.

The staring and giggling start as soon as they walk in. They order their food and within minutes, a fry full of ketchup lands in Tanya's hair. She claps her hand to her head and snaps around, looking for the culprit. When she notices Mark and his sidekick Danny, she glowers at them like some kind of medieval dragon and mutters under her breath. She wipes at the ketchup smeared in her hair.

"Good one!" she yells while rolling her eyes.

Tanya's mother doesn't seem to notice. Their order is up and a minute later they're out the door. The room fills with fits of laughter coming from the table where Mark and Danny sit with a couple of girls. I watch Tanya and her mom get in the car.

"This totally sucks," I tell Ahmed as they drive away.

"What? Tanya?" Ahmed asks as he shovels fry after fry in his mouth. "I know," he manages to say when he comes up for air. I take a bite from my salad and shake my head.

"Dude, you okay?" Ahmed asks. I chew on the watery mess in my mouth. "Oh . . . woops, sorry. This isn't cool for you, is it?"

"You think?" I say.

"Right." He shoves the last bit of apple fritters in his mouth and slurps the last of his Coke, "ah fun," he manages through his grotesquely full mouth. He swallows. "Sorry, all done," he repeats.

"Thanks. You can make it up to me by trading lockers," I tell him.

"Hell no! Tanya Bate is anthrax. Get near her and you're asking for a death sentence."

I groan. "Don't remind me, man. You got room in your locker?" I ask, willing to be tardy for every class and serve detentions from now until the end of the school year since Ahmed's locker isn't near any of my classes.

"Yeah, right! Wait . . . I didn't tell you! Oh my God, I can't believe I haven't told you!" Ahmed starts twitching like he just stuck his finger in an outlet. "Guess who my locker partner is? Janie Hass, man! Freaking Janie Haas," Ahmed says with a grin and puts two fingers to his head to resemble devil horns, "and Katrina basically has rights to it, too because you know how girls are." Ahmed shakes his head and stares off into space. "This may be it, Chuckie, the start of a whole new outlook. These girls will reinstate my faith in womankind." He sighs, presumably at some fantasy that involves him and the two hottest senior girls in our school. I can't believe it. It totally figures.

"You realize that *you* are Janie's Tanya Bate," I tell him.

"Doesn't matter, my man. By the end of the year, those two foxy honeys will be putty in my hands. You think it's a sign that Janie Hass's name includes the word ass? Gonna be a great year with the ladies!" He is beaming like a little kid who just got a puppy for Christmas, delivered into his arms by Santa himself.

I eye Ahmed's remnants of fries. "Man, why did this have to happen to me?" I ask him. "I had plans, you know? This was supposed to be my year."

"Shake it off, my man, and whatever, just carry your books."

"Right! You know how many books I'll have this year? I already have five for my two AP classes."

Ahmed whistles low and long, "That's what you get for being stupid smart, my man."

I notice Mark heading over to our table.

"Hey, Chunks, sorry about the shit earlier today," he says. "No hard feelings, right?"

"Right," I mumble even though I notice I have a clear shot at his jaw and nothing would please me more than to land a punch on his smug face.

"Come on, that was hilarious! When Danny suggested it to me, I was like, hell yeah, man, we gotta do it! And for a split second, I thought about backing down when I found out you were her locker buddy, but . . ." His laughter comes harder, verging on uncontrollable as he tries to finish his sentence. "We just *had* to do it, man," he finally finishes.

I hold up my hand and nod. He gives me a hard slap on the back. "I knew you'd understand, Chunks. And don't worry, the next one won't be so bad," he says and walks away.

Great.

CHAPTER THREE

The following Thursday is my birthday, which only reminds me of last year, even though I had truly spent most of my time blocking it out of my mind since then. Mom always used to make me skip school on my birthday, declaring that how in the world could I be expected to pay attention to a bunch of boring teachers on a day meant to celebrate my life?

When I was younger, skipping school with Mom had actually been cool because she always had something planned. A movie, a beach trip, the Fun Zone, and one time we went bowling. But that was when it had stopped being cool. It was the year I turned nine and our bowling game ended with her flipping out because the guy at the counter overcharged her for the games we played. They kept arguing back and forth, and she caused a big scene that made me hate bowling forever.

I'd seen Mom get angry in public before and noticed how she sometimes acted out if other people rubbed her the wrong way, but usually they would just give up. Not this time. This time, each nerve in my body stood on high alert, warning me that something bad was going to happen. It wouldn't have been that big of a deal if the place had been empty. As it was, though, there was a large group of league players practicing that day, and Mom's yelling drew a lot of attention to herself. People were staring at us, but she just kept getting angrier about the five dollars the guy insisted she still owed. He wouldn't give us back our shoes until she paid it. She looked at the guy like she wanted to strangle him, getting angrier and angrier to the point of literally shaking. But the guy seemed to be enjoying it all and at some point actually chuckled.

I swallowed hard and closed my eyes. My heart raced as I waited for Mom to go ape shit. But instead, she stopped yelling. Just like that. I opened one eye just in time to see her slam five dollars on the table and say, "Here you go jerkoff. Now give me back our shoes." She spat those last words out hard and slow. I breathed a sigh of relief.

Mom took him by surprise, which is probably why he made the mistake of giving us back our regular shoes before Mom handed over our rental shoes. One by one, Mom started chucking them at the guy's head. She yelled at me to make a run for it as the league players started coming toward us and the shoe guy cursed her out. By the time we got to the car, Mom couldn't stop laughing, but I didn't think it was funny at all. I remember worrying all night if the guy behind the counter was going to find us or call the cops. We never went back again, and I never told Dad about it. Between the laughs and the insistence that the guy deserved it, Mom told me not to.

It would seem that nothing could top the bowling shoes incident, but last year Mom really outdid herself.

As usual, she had insisted I stay home, especially because *seventeen is your last official year of being a kid, Charlie! We should go to an amusement park! We can ride roller coasters all day!* she had said, but the anxiety and dread that came along with Mom's unpredictable behavior, and the idea of spending the whole day with her was too much.

"I can call your teachers and tell them we have some kind of emergency," she said over huge Belgian waffles she'd made for my special birthday breakfast.

I shook my head no and made up some lame excuse about a huge test I couldn't miss. And before she could come up with a way to keep me home, I was out the door. It quickly became one of the worst decisions I've ever made.

Most of the day went smoothly . . . a little too smoothly. A quiz I was actually supposed to take in history got postponed, and we had a sub in another class who had us watch a video. I was thoroughly enjoying my good day until I realized these were signs. Something was not right.

I could have just chocked it up to luck, and maybe this had been the universe's way of saying *Happy birthday, Charlie, I know your life sucks, so the cosmic forces and I have come together and we hope you have a nice day. Enjoy!* ☺. But I knew better. By lunchtime, my stomach was in knots, with that feeling your gut gives you when it's saying, *Hang the fuck on, brother! Some stuff is about to go down*—and all too soon I realized the universe is really a sadistic bitch that's been setting me up for the biggest birthday fuck ever.

I can still picture Mom perfectly on that day. Well, at first I didn't quite see her so much as the insane amount of helium balloons that were headed toward the front office, bouncing off people and taking up most of the walkway. She reminded me of an old underwear commercial where these guys dress up like fruit and one of them is covered in purple balloons to look like a gigantic cluster of grapes. But Mom was three gigantic clusters of grapes in Technicolor.

"Hi, honey!" she yelled from down the hall, waving, and peering around the balloons. People laughed and pointed at me as Mom started making her way toward me and Ahmed.

"Holy shit," I whispered to Ahmed.

"Wow. Okay, just relax, no biggie," Ahmed said. No biggie? Had he seen what I saw? This was a freaking humongous, insane biggie!

"Surprise!" she yelled. More laughter, more pointing.

"Mom . . ."

"Isn't this great! I wanted to make it special just for you. After all, it is your last year as a kid, officially!" she gushed and then she did the only thing that could have possibly made her plan worse than it already was. She cleared her throat and started singing. My blood raced up to my face like the red stuff in a thermometer on a sweltering day. I felt like I was going to die. People laughed harder. I remember how incredibly loud her voice had sounded and how I wished I could magically transform into a gnat and fly away. I remember thinking this couldn't possibly be happening and how long could the seemingly innocent freakin' birthday song possibly be? Since then I've figured out that it takes approximately fourteen seconds to sing "Happy Birthday" to someone, but it felt like an entire hour. And I really hate that song now.

". . . dear Charlie . . ."

More people who were laughing and pointing and staring at me formed around Mom, Ahmed, and me. And to his credit, Ahmed didn't even pretend to not know me.

". . . to you . . ." Thunderous applauses and deafening whistles exploded from the crowd as Mom finished, and she was so damn pleased with herself that her face was beaming. She looked like she just sang at Carnegie Hall and didn't even notice how my heart had stopped beating, how my lungs didn't work, how I was actually dying of humiliation.

She gave a bow and thanked the crowd, and they cheered her on even more. A nervous teacher who had seen everything finally broke it up by announcing loudly that everyone should get to class. Very slowly did the cheers die down and the crowd finally dispersed. I heard a few whispers and lingering giggles as everyone left the Fuck Your Son's Birthday Show.

"I was going to try and convince them to let me take these to your class and sing to you so you'd really be surprised, but, oh well. This works too. Here you go, honey!" she said. Was she serious? Yes, she was. I couldn't move. I was the Tin Man left out in the rain.

"Charlie! Take them," she said, laughing. "Told you I was gonna do something special!"

I lifted a rusted arm and took them before she said

anything else. I stood there like an idiot as she grinned from ear to ear like she'd just done the most spectacular thing in the world. I wanted to kill her. But the bell rang and I had to get to my next class, so I told her I had to go.

"Okay, see you later. I'm making something special for dinner." She winked and left me with the big mess she had just made. I couldn't believe it, and yet, I could.

Now, my options were to walk around like balloon boy the rest of the day or pop approximately thirty balloons and return home empty-handed, which would require some kind of explanation for Mom. Either option seemed ridiculous, which was why I was grateful when Ahmed, wonderful remedial-reading, general math, Ceramics I, II, and III–taking Ahmed, came up with the most brilliant idea in the world.

"That's a lot of freaking balloons," he said, "a *lot*."

"I know."

"It's too bad, really just too bad," he said.

"I can't walk around like this," I said, my voice shaking and not catching his drift.

"I mean, it's just too bad," he said again.

"What the hell are you talking about!" I yelled, dumping all my frustration onto him. "What's too bad?" I said, "That my mom is insane? That I look like an idiot? That this," I said as I raised my fist holding all the balloon strings, "is supposed to brighten my day?"

"Well, yes, all those things are bad," he said, "but what's really bad, really, really bad," he continues, "is how some dumbass is going to bump into you and make you lose your grip on those things, and how they'll just

. . . float away." And even though I'm totally straight, I remember thinking how much I loved Ahmed and that he was quite possibly the best guy on earth.

I was suddenly eternally indebted to both Ahmed and the architectural genius who designed open school campuses. Instead of one huge building, there are a bunch of small buildings that each house a row of lockers and several classrooms. Outdoor walkways connect them all together to form one semi-eerie minicompound. It's a total bitch in the heat (especially when you're over two hundred pounds) and sucks when it rains, but insanely perfect when your mom shows up with a trillion balloons that you have to get rid of—fast. Ahmed gave me a light push and I opened my hand. We grinned at each other. The bundle of tangled strings slipped through my fingers easily.

"Now you don't have to lie," he said as we watched them go higher and higher. Despite the horridness of what I had just experienced, I had to admit, they looked pretty spectacular against the blue sky. The wind carried them away, and we watched as they got smaller and smaller and finally disappeared.

"Yeah," I said as I watched my problem float away, and I remember wishing all problems were that easy to get rid of.

Today, though, Mom's gone. There's no arguing about me staying home—no crazy-ass balloons to embarrass me with. I'm glad I don't have to think about her.

Dad comes downstairs right before I head out. "Sport, hey! Happy Birthday!" he yells. He hugs me and slaps me on the back a few times. "I can't believe it. Eighteen years ago today, your mom and I . . ." He stops suddenly and looks away. It's weird how we can't bring her up when she's not here. He shrugs it off. "Well, I just want you to know I'm proud of you," he says.

"For being another year older?"

"No, I mean, yeah. You're growing up, Charlie, and you really know how to handle yourself. Look at you," he says, "you weren't happy with your weight and you changed it." *Wasn't that because you made me?* "Anyway, you're really something, you know? In lots of ways, you have more will than I do."

Dad is getting a little too sentimental. Even though what he's saying is nice, I don't feel like partaking in this feel-good moment. In the back of my mind, I can't help but wonder what he'd be saying or how he'd be looking at me right now if I were still fat.

"Thanks, Dad," I say a little awkwardly as I gather my backpack. Ahmed is here and honks his car horn.

"We'll celebrate later, okay?" he calls out as I head out the door.

"Sure," I call back.

When I get into the Roller Skate, Ahmed throws a cigar at me and a *Best of Dean Martin* CD.

"Happy eighteenth, player! Now you can officially vote, buy cigars, and purchase . . ." He clears his throat and adjusts his tie in true Sammy Davis Jr. fashion. "Gentlemen's magazines." He raises his eyebrows and laughs. I laugh too and thank him for the CD and cigar even though I neither smoke nor can stand the smell of cigars. Dean Martin is pretty cool, though. "And since all you ever do is listen to your iPod, we can keep this in my car," he says, plucking the CD right out of my hand and tearing off the wrapper.

"Thanks a lot," I say, not surprised because pretty much every gift Ahmed has given me has found its way back to him. I put the cigar in my backpack as the Roller Skate zips us off to school.

•••

The day goes as usual and then during drama, the very class I'm trying to switch out of, I get called down to the guidance office to discuss a schedule change.

My guidance counselor, Ms. Sheldon, wears a bright green shirt that hurts my eyes. She has short, gray hair that resembles a buzz cut, and she wears red-framed glasses attached to an elaborate bejeweled chain. In the four years I've been at this school, this is the first time I've met her. She is happy to meet me, she says, and why haven't I been in to chat with her before? I shrug my shoulders since there's really no way to answer that question. I look around and notice the many pictures of students and big bubbly girl-writing on handmade cards decorating her office. Apparently, stopping in to chat is something lots of other students have done.

"So this is your senior year! Are you excited?" I nod.

"And look at you, with all these AP classes and a, oh my gosh, a 3.8 grade point average? That's impressive. Really, congratulations," she says, turning to me and smiling. I fiddle with my watch.

"I do notice one small setback, though," she continues, "no extracurricular activities, Charles, and that's something colleges are definitely looking for these days." She looks at me over her glasses.

"Yeah," I say and take a deep breath. It's not like I hadn't thought of that before.

"Why?" she asks.

"Just . . ." I shrug my shoulders. "I don't know," I tell her, which is entirely false. The truth is that fat doesn't do extracurricular activities. Fat always gets in the way. Fat makes you stay home so people don't notice you or say shit behind your extra wide back.

She nods. "Well, your grades are fabulous, so maybe if you join some clubs this year, you'll still have no problem getting into the college of your choice, which brings me to this. You want out of drama, I see?" she says, looking at the schedule change request form I filled out after school on the first day.

"Yep."

"Well, you're not the first one, but I'll tell you this, I think you should seriously consider keeping it. Staying in drama might offer a great extracurricular opportunity for you."

I shift in my seat uncomfortably. *No, just get me out of there.* I don't want to be talked into staying in the class, but she keeps going on and on, and the more she talks, the more I sink into the quicksand of compliance. I can't say no now. She's been talking nonstop for the past fifteen minutes.

". . . not even on stage, but you can do some work backstage and . . ."

First Tanya Bate . . . now this.

". . . love to see a student challenge himself, try new

things, and it might even be a great topic for a college essay. So, what do you say, Charles?" I say screw you, lady.

"Sure," comes out instead.

"Great! I'm proud of you. You'll see, it'll probably end up being your favorite class." Doubt it.

Ten minutes later, I'm still reeling as I stumble back to class with no schedule change. How do they do that? She looked nice, and yet, the old bat had somehow duped me into staying in drama. I decide to skip the rest of class and go sit on a bench, mentally composing my bio to post on FML.

As I sit feeling sorry for myself, thinking what a crappy birthday this is turning out to be, Charlotte VanderKleaton appears out of nowhere and walks past me. I sit still and stop breathing, hoping she won't notice the loser sitting here with absolutely nothing to do. I stare at the cracks on the ground until she is a safe distance away. I see her going in the direction of the drama room.

Wait. The drama room? And . . . she's got her backpack, so she's obviously not just running some stupid errand. What's that in her hand? . . . a crisp, new schedule? It's not possible, and yet, there she goes headed toward the drama room.

I see her hand reach for the heavy classroom door and a minute later she disappears into the room. Charlotte VanderKleaton is now in drama. Sixth period drama with me. Sixth period drama that I tried to get out of. Sixth period drama that the wonderful Ms. Sheldon had the good sense to talk me into keeping. I look up and smile. I jump off the bench and head to what is now officially my favorite class. Happy freakin' birthday to me!

When I get to the door, I take a deep breath. Actually, I take several deep breaths since I start to feel overwhelmed, but I put my hand on the handle and pull. And the door opens and reveals the heavenly sight of Charlotte VanderKleaton, sitting in the seat right next to mine. My ears fill with the arena sound of a thousand fans cheering, and I kind of feel like I might fall over.

I don't know how I make it to my desk, but I do, so I sit down and concentrate on breathing for the remaining five minutes of class. I try not to look her way, but I can't help it. She looks over at me at the same time.

"Hi," she says.

My God, she speaks. I'm unable to answer or make a sound.

"So, how much have I missed? Just got my schedule changed," she says. Her voice makes my body pulse with adrenaline. She stares and I realize she's waiting for an answer, but I can feel my throat closing up.

My hand flies up in an attempt to dismiss the whole thing in a cool, "forget about it," kind of way and I try to make a no-big-deal face, but as I'm doing it, I can feel that it somehow went very, very wrong. Most likely I look as if I'm constipated and swatting an imaginary fly. Nice.

She laughs and says, "O-kay," and then opens her notebook. She starts doodling as the teacher goes on about some play.

I try to breathe normally, but it's impossible. She must hear my heavy breathing. My whole body is very aware that she's sitting next to me. A whole school year sitting next to Charlotte VanderKleaton. And I don't have to worry about squishing into the desk or excessive sweating or clothes being stuck in my fat rolls. I can sit here, not fat, next to Charlotte VanderKleaton and be normal, I think. I look at her again, and she smiles back.

The bell rings, and I'm relieved because if it hadn't rang at that precise moment, I would still be in awe of her complete and utter awesomeness. She gets up and walks out the door with the rest of the class. I try to recover.

"Do you need something?" Mrs. C asks and I realize I'm the only student left in the room.

"No, thanks," I tell her, gathering my stuff and tripping over my own feet on the way out.

After class, I'm in such a good mood that I head toward my locker. I had avoided it all week. Since Ahmed basically screwed me for Janie and Katrina, I decided that carrying my books this year wouldn't be so bad. But already my shoulders were sore and I knew I would eventually have to abort the plan. Why not now? After being in such close proximity of Charlotte, I feel like Hercules: invincible, and ready to conquer the three-headed hound of Hades known as Tanya Bate.

Even from down the hall, I can see Tanya's fuzzy head as she shoves books into our locker. I stop for a minute, waiting for her to leave, but Tanya takes her sweet-ass time, so I head over to her.

"Can I help you?" she asks, giving me a dirty look when I stop in front of our locker.

"I, uh, this is my locker, too," I tell her.

She surveys me, her big owl eyes taking me in from top to bottom. Was she serious? Was she actually sizing me up?

"So," she says finally, "you decided to bite the bullet and show up. What? Do I scare you?" She opens her eyes wider and wider until, in fact, she does look pretty scary, since her superthick glasses already make her eyes look huge.

"No, I just . . ."

"Yeah, yeah, save it, chump. I know. Books get heavy. I hear it every year. Anyway, just don't get in my way and I won't get in yours and we'll get along fine. Don't worry, it's not like we're gonna be friends or anything. I know you have your precious social life to worry about, what with your new makeover and everything," she says looking me up and down.

I feel weird and people turn and look at us, making me wish I could crawl into a hole and hide. I feel like reminding everyone that we don't get to choose our locker partners.

"Sshhh," I hiss, hoping she will lower her voice.

"And don't expect these kinds of pleasantries in the future," she goes on, "I do have things to do and places to be." Oh man, this girl is a total freak.

"See you whenever," she says and slams the locker shut, even though it's obvious that I have to use it. She whips her frizzy hair in my face as she turns to leave. It brushes up against my mouth. I gag.

Once I recover, I open the locker again only to find that Tanya has taken the top space, leaving only the dreaded bottom empty. I drop to the floor and start unloading my books, trying to figure out how to best avoid Tanya Bate for the rest of the year. But then I think of Charlotte, and suddenly, Tanya Bate (who, incidentally, smells like peanut butter) is a distant memory.

• • •

That night, Dad, Ahmed, and I go to Fresca's for my birthday dinner. It has a salad bar, soups, sandwiches, and a fruit smoothie and frozen yogurt station. When we sit at the table, Dad takes out an envelope and pushes it my way. Money slips out when I open it.

"Sorry, Sport," he says, embarrassed, "but I didn't really know what you wanted and I figured you could always use cash." My jaw drops as I pick up the one-hundred-dollar bill.

"Hell, yeah!" Ahmed yells, "Oh, sorry, Mr. Grisner," he says, looking over at Dad.

"I hope that's okay," Dad says, looking back at me. "I know your eighteenth is a big deal and all . . ." He looks around Fresca's and seems to be having second thoughts. "Maybe we should've gone somewhere else."

I don't know if it's because my plans of getting Charlotte VanderKleaton are somehow not as impossible as I had thought or because part of me feels like I owe that all to Dad, but I suddenly feel like cutting him a break, at least for now.

I look around the place and say, "This is great, Dad, really. And thanks." I hold up the hundred-dollar bill. "I can definitely use this," I say, hoping I'm convincing.

A small wave of relief comes over Dad's face. Ahmed

cracks some jokes on how he needs a new pair of wing tips, and I bust his chops on how many he already has all the while trying to convince myself that this no-big-deal kind of celebration is exactly what I wanted—and trying to forget that as much as Mom's presence on my birthday always made me hate my birthday, this was the first time she'd missed it.

CHAPTER FOUR

Over the weekend, Ahmed and I hang out at the local mini mall. Lots of people from school hang out there, especially on Friday and Saturday nights since it has a movie theater. I keep hoping I'll see Charlotte since I've deserted the run-bys past her house. I'm pretty sure now that we have a class together, she'll catch on to my stalker-like tendencies (plus I never feel like running anymore).

But I don't see her all weekend long, and by Sunday night I'm going through Charlotte withdrawal. I'm dying for Monday to come.

I look at the pile of dirty laundry in the corner of my room and gather up my clothes to throw into the washer. Then I wonder, maybe I could do something more. I mean, is it possible I might have more to offer than just clean clothes? Ahmed's talk on male grooming rings in my ears. "Listen, Charlie, ain't no shame in putting a little effort into your appearance. Just because you're a guy doesn't mean you gotta walk around with crud on your teeth and nappy hair. Girls appreciate attention to details. Look at the old cats. They always looked sharp."

I go check myself out in the bathroom mirror. I still

have a big moon pie of a face. Okay, so maybe it's slightly slimmer. I had lost thirty pounds, after all, and I don't jiggle like I used to. I also wasn't obese anymore, (though, technically, I had, in fact, fallen in that category). I was pretty surprised since I didn't think I looked obese. But a five-foot-ten male at 235 pounds qualifies as just that. At least now I could pass for one of those slightly big jocks—with what suddenly looks like the beginning of a huge zit on my lower jaw.

I smile. Maybe I could whiten my teeth. Or maybe get a haircut. Dad was always telling me to get a haircut, but that's because he's so clean cut. I take out the gel and slather my hair, trying to get that cool, messy look. But it just looks like an alien shit on my head and I'm trying too hard, which I am. I decide to not shave for the next couple of days in hopes that it will hide the zit and give me that hung-over musician look. Perhaps a tattoo would complete the look. Maybe then I'd look big and bad instead of just big.

When Monday morning finally does come, I practically jump out of bed. My mornings are pretty heavy, and now, since I'm dying for sixth period to roll around, miserably long. I start getting jittery ten minutes into first, and by the time I'm walking to sixth period, I feel like I'm going into a diabetic shock. But, in the end, I finally get my fix.

Drama.

I'm already sitting at my desk, anticipating her arrival, but I pretend not to notice as she gets into the seat next to me.

"Hey," she says breathlessly. She has said hey to me

like this every day since she got her schedule changed. I live for these heys.

I nod and smile like I usually do.

"Don't you talk?" she asks this time, laughing. I shift in my seat trying to adjust myself.

I nod and smile. She laughs again. I rack my brain for something to say, *anything, my God, how could I have gotten this far in life without any conversational skills? Come on* . . . But she's got bubble gum in her mouth, and she chews it so sexy that it's all I can focus on. I can't even think straight.

She blows a bubble and sucks it in real fast and little tiny popping sounds go off in her mouth. She smiles and nods like she just did some awesome trick. I laugh, but it comes out like a snort. She laughs too and fake snorts, which despite embarrassing me, also makes me laugh harder. And when Mrs. C starts class, we both face forward repressing stupid giggles. Mrs. C gives us a few warning looks, and finally we settle down.

I sense Charlotte sneaking a few glances my way. I try to find something to do with my hands. I pray she doesn't notice Gynormo-Zit, which is only slightly camouflaged by the peach fuzz I woke up with this morning. I put my left elbow on my desk, and rest my face on my hand, and while this does successfully hide Gynormo, it means I can't look at her without being obvious about it. I try to catch a few glimpses out of the corner of my eye, and each time I look over, she's looking my way too, smiling back. But then, I'm so paranoid about the freakin' zit I can't even enjoy the whole experience.

These are the times I wish I could draw so that at

least I could look superbusy and like I don't notice her looking my way because I'm such a dark, brooding artist and all that matters is my art. I have to find something to do.

I open my notebook with my free hand and decide to attempt to draw anyway. But I don't know what to draw, so I start tapping on my paper instead, pretending I'm thinking really hard about something. But before I know it, the pencil flies out of my hand and across the room and falls right in front of Mrs. C, whose eyes open wide and look at me with that look teachers have that says, *one more thing and your ass is out of here.*

I look over at Charlotte, whose dark eyes sparkle with glee. She's really thinking all this is hilarious. I finally settle on just keeping my eyes straight ahead and pretending she's not right next to me. It's impossible.

"All right, get started," Mrs. C says and I realize I haven't heard a word she's said and have exactly no idea what it is we're supposed to get started on.

"Come on," Charlotte says, turning her desk so it faces mine as everyone else starts scattering around the room.

"What? What are we supposed to be doing?" I finally stutter, still in disbelief that she's shifting her desk toward me.

"Weren't you listening?" she asks. I have no clue how to respond. She's sitting there, waiting for an answer again. My brain tweaks out and comes up with all the possible responses I can give, and transmits everything to my mouth where all of it meshes together and has the potential to come out of my mouth in incomprehensible stutters. This, unfortunately, conjures up memories of Porky Pig from *Looney Tunes*, which is about the last thing I want to think about—a stuttering pig. Charlotte smiles and starts cracking up. I feel my face turning red.

"You're so funny," she says, even though I'm not trying to be and feel like an idiot. I laugh nervously.

"So, I'm Charlotte." *As if I didn't know.* "And you are . . . ?" She looks at me and I know I'm supposed to say something. "Hello? What's your name?" she asks. *Speak, dumbass, speak!*

"Charlie," I manage, but I think it comes out funny. I cough and clear my throat.

"Charlie," she says like she's never heard or said the name before. "Okay, Charlie, so we're supposed to pick a play, summarize it, design the set on graph paper, and then make a small-scale model of it. She's going to give us class time for the next couple of weeks to work on it. Geez, she was talking for like twenty minutes. Preoccupied with something?"

I shrug. *Only you and your awesomeness.* She studies my face, then twirls a lock of her hair around her finger "You look familiar." She narrows her eyes a little. "Didn't you used to run around the neighborhood or something?"

Oh my God, she did notice me. She must think I'm a stalker freak, or worse, she realizes I'm the fat kid that didn't wave back. Any minute now, her face will get that disgusted look and she'll get up and refuse to work with me. She stares, waiting, still twirling that lock of red hair.

I nod. "Uh, yeah. I mean, I did. But I had to stop. Knee injury." Wonderful. The little conversational skills I have finally kick in and all I can do is come up with a lame-ass lie. What the hell did I know about knee injuries? What if she asks me about it?

"That sucks," she says. I wait for her to ask me more, to demand proof of the alleged injury, but she just smiles and says, "So, what play do you want to do? *Romeo and Juliet?*" She raises an eyebrow and smiles. Then waits for an answer again.

She must be joking, right? I mean, Shakespeare would shit bricks if he saw someone like me in the role of Romeo. But Charlotte would be a perfect Juliet. I read the play and watched the movie freshman year, but honestly, all I remember about it is that Romeo and Juliet both die, but before that, I'm pretty sure they do it.

"Whatever," I answer, "your choice."

She laughs and I'm not sure if she's laughing at me or what, but then she says, "Okay, I'll be right back," and tosses her hair over her shoulder before heading toward Mrs. C's library of plays.

I'm suddenly realizing that she might be using that tone. The tone of voice girls use when they know something guys don't. When they ask questions they already know the answers to. When they're . . . is that flirting? I've never actually had a girl flirt with me, and I've definitely never flirted back with anyone. I'm not sure I even know how to flirt. But more importantly, *is* she flirting? Does she like me? Or is she just being nice?

She looks back at me a couple of times. I pretend not to notice, but now there's a giddiness inside me, swelling and gathering force, threatening to come out in a wild, mad-scientist kind of laugh. I force it down and try not to appear too anxious.

She returns exuberant and bubbly with a play in her hand. She whoopees and yays, which is so annoying in some girls, but absolutely perfect in her. She tells me this is the only play in the world worth reading. I look at the cover, which reads *A Streetcar Named Desire*. I've never heard of it.

"This is the best play ever!" she gushes. "Stanley Kowalski is so . . . so powerful and moving." She stares at the cover. I gather that the angry, shirtless guy on it must be Stanley. I'm suddenly irrationally jealous of him.

"But Blanche, poor Blanche. She's such a weirdo and pretty annoying. She can't do anything for herself. I can't stand people like that, who *need* other people. It's so . . . wimpy, know what I mean?" I nod. Yes, I knew exactly what she meant. She starts to fill me in on the play, but I already know I'll read it anyway. We're talking about what set to recreate (actually, she's talking and I'm just watching and listening), when the bell rings, ending the greatest class in my whole academic career.

"You better read it," she says, pointing to the play.

"I will, definitely," I say with a big grin. I'm not so keen on reading a book about some muscle-head guy Charlotte has a literary crush on, but if she wants me to read it, I'll read it.

"Okay." She smiles back. "Well, you could just watch the movie. I mean, it's pretty much the same." She gathers up her books, flashes me one last smile, and leaves, not realizing that I would walk over hot coals for her if she asked me. Even if she didn't.

I straighten out her desk and gather up my books, still stunned over what has just transpired in the last hour. Again, I'm the last one to leave.

The walk to Ahmed's car is different today. A hint of fall is in the breeze; the air smells fresher, the world looks brighter, and I can't wipe the stupid grin off my face.

"What the hell is up with you?" Ahmed asks, looking up from his phone. He's leaning on the Roller Skate, texting.

I shake my head, trying to clear it and suddenly I worry that what I think just happened didn't really happen. Maybe I'm making too much of it. Maybe I totally misinterpreted the best forty-five minutes of my life. I tell Ahmed everything as soon as we get in the car, to see what he thinks, making extra sure I haven't overelaborated or left anything out.

"Oh no, watch out! Chuckie's a p-p-p-piiimp!" he cries out.

"Shut the hell up!" I tell him. The windows of the Roller Skate are down as we zip out of the parking lot.

"She digs you," Ahmed says. "Enjoy it, man! Lap it up like an itty-bitty puppy dying of thirst." Ahmed makes slurping sounds and starts cracking up. I laugh and look out the window, the car zooming at what feels like perilous speeds. I change Ahmed's Sinatra CD to the Beastie Boys. I turn up the volume and we act like the best white boy rappers to hit the east side since Mike D, Ad-Rock, and MCA, although technically we wouldn't be a white boy group since I'm white and

Ahmed is Turkish. Anyway, Ahmed has abandoned his Rat Pack persona for the moment and is his full spazzo self—dancing, rapping, and flashing peace signs to cars next to us. It makes me crack up the whole ride home, and I can't remember the last time I felt this good.

CHAPTER FIVE

The next month is the best one of my life, despite the following:
- Dad is never home because of work.
- Mom is never home because she's Mom.
- It's officially the longest she's ever been gone.
- I haven't lost any more weight. In fact, I've gained two pounds.
- Drama has turned into the most humiliating experience of my life.

So, technically, yes, I get to drool over Charlotte for the entire class period every day. But not only do I have to get up in front of the whole class and recite monologues, I have to get up in front of Charlotte and recite monologues, and I'm terrible. It's basically three minutes of pure terror and tongue twisters that just make everyone else feel sorry for me. And, of course, as it turns out, Charlotte is a pretty terrific actress and makes everyone else look bad. Every day, all I can do is dread/look forward to sixth period. But things are a lot better when we get more class time to work on the project. Since everything else in my life sucks, the only thing that keeps me going is the time I spend with

Charlotte in drama. I read *A Streetcar Named Desire* and watched the movie right after Charlotte told me about it. She's right, it is a pretty good play, but I can't figure out if I hate Stanley because he's a first-rate jerk or because the sight of him on the cover of the playbook makes Charlotte swoon. And I don't know if this makes me one of the drama kids or not, but I finally get the whole *STELLA!* thing.

"So, you ready for your drama presentation today?" Dad asks me as I come into the kitchen on one of the rare mornings I catch him before he leaves for work. He's always had to travel for work, but lately he's had to a lot more, which means late nights and early mornings at the office when he is in town.

"Uh, yeah, I guess. I mean, at least it's a partner thing, you know?"

"Yeah, takes the pressure off. Well, I'm sure you'll do fine, Sport," he says as he sets his coffee mug in the sink.

"Thanks, Dad. Oh, and your turn or mine?" I ask him since I can't remember which one of us is supposed to fix dinner tonight. We'd fallen into this routine of who could fix the best tasting but still healthy meals since I got back from fat camp. It was Dad's lame idea, and I hadn't really been trying lately, but figured I could do it to make things a little less tense around here.

"Probably another late night, so don't worry about me," he says. Ahmed honks the horn. "Good luck," he says as I walk out the door.

All day my stomach is in knots as I anticipate the presentation in drama. I'm pretty nervous, but Charlotte is calm as usual when I walk into class. She smiles as I take deep breaths and try to relax. The anxiety from waiting is almost as bad as the actual standing in front of the class, and just when I absolutely can't take the waiting anymore, Mrs. C finally calls us up. As I start summarizing the play, my voice has the usual weird shakiness whenever I get up here. No matter how much I try, I can't make myself sound normal. I get tangled up in the story line and then for whatever reason I start rambling on and on about Tennessee Williams, at which point I notice people starting to doodle and scrape gum off their shoes. Those who are still paying attention look like I just asked them to explain the latest quantum physics theories complete with formulas and illustrations. I'm choking.

"What Charlie means is . . . ," Charlotte cuts in. She easily explains the rest of the play, leaving out some key events, but it's still way better than all my stupid rambling. Mrs. C nods her head as she listens and scribbles notes.

Charlotte goes on to explain our design, why we chose the colors we chose for the set, what kind of lighting we would incorporate, how it all adds to the mood, etc., with very little help from me. When I do speak, I feel like a parrot, echoing things she's already said.

"Good," Mrs. C says when we're done, "so, what did you guys think of Blanche?" she asks.

"I can't stand her," Charlotte answers immediately.

Mrs. C tilts her head to one side. "Most people can't," she says. "What about you, Charlie?"

"Well, she *is* kind of annoying, but . . ." I shrug my shoulders, not knowing how to finish my thought.

"Go on," Mrs. C suggests.

But Charlotte quickly takes over. "Come on, she's basically this nymphomaniac who is superold, like thirty or forty or something and, you know . . . actually hooks up with one of her students. I mean who does that? And then, oh yeah, then comes on to that other teenage newspaper boy." Hoots and hollers echo from our now revived class as well as a couple of *ewww's*.

"And then she's a total compulsive liar, too—lying to anyone and everyone, especially poor, stupid big Mitch. I hate that. I mean, he's such a good guy, you know? And she just takes complete advantage of him. So, I think considering all that, you know, she's actually worse than Stanley." Mrs. C raises her eyebrows. I think we just took a wrong turn.

"I mean, okay, Stanley might seem like a jerk and all, but at least he's honest, you know? I appreciate that. Blanche just pretends to be something she's not. She's definitely got some issues," Charlotte concludes.

"Exactly the point, Charlotte. She's got issues. And does that justify what Stanley does to her in the end?" Mrs. C asks. She clicks her tongue in a semidisapproving, semigenuinely interested in what we have to say kind of way.

Charlotte shrugs. "She sort of put herself in that position," she says. But I don't know what to say. I don't know what the right answer is.

"Stanley breaks Blanche," Mrs. C says, perhaps thinking we didn't fully understand the play. "He knows he can, and he does," she continues. "Is that okay?"

Charlotte shrugs. "I think she was already broken,"

she says, without much sympathy. They go back and forth for a while, but there's really no shaking Charlotte and how much she dislikes Blanche.

Mrs. C looks at me. "What about you, Charlie, what do you think?" she asks.

This whole talk about Blanche, what she deserves, what she doesn't deserve, and how much she lies, makes my head feel stuffed. The room feels like it's rocking under my feet, but no one else seems to notice the mini earthquake, so I try to ignore it. But the truth is, I both hate and feel bad for Blanche. She's weak, needy, and incredibly deceptive. I kind of get how she suffocates everyone in her life, but the reasons she's fucked up are hard to define. The way nobody cares about her really sucks, so you kind of feel bad for her. I guess I also understand how people sometimes feel the need to lie because the truth is so bad. I feel the floor tremble again.

"I agree with Charlotte," I finally mumble.

Mrs. C looks at us the way adults do, right before they justify your responses to pure teenage stupidity.

"Well," she says and sighs, "we could go on about this forever, but we have more presentations. Thank you, Charlotte and Charlie. All right, next we have . . ."

Charlotte and I walk back to our seats. "Good job," she whispers. Was she being sarcastic? Or did she really not notice the way I clammed up or how Mrs. C just looked at us? We sit down and the next pair goes on about some other play. Charlotte scribbles a note and passes it to me.

I think we got an A, what do you think?

Yeah, Maybe.

Anyway, it's been really cool working on this with you. And I was thinking, a bunch of us are going on a Halloween hayride on Thursday night. Wanna go?

Did I want to go on a hayride with Charlotte VanderKleaton? Did the sun shine? Was water wet? Suddenly I don't give a crap about Blanche DuBois. I look over at Charlotte and offer her what I hope is a casual nod. She gives me a thumbs-up. And just like that, life is good.

The bell rings just as another group is in midpresentation. Mrs. C says we'll continue tomorrow and everyone rushes out.

"So, the hayride is on Thursday. It's supposed to be really fun," Charlotte says. We stand outside the drama room. Even though we've been working on the presentation together and I've been in class with her for over a month now, I still feel weird around her. There are a hundred thoughts going through my head right now. Was she really asking me to go somewhere with her? My mouth doesn't work. *Don't mess this up. Act cool.*

Just speak.

"Cool," I say.

"Cool," she says. Yes, this is all very, very cool. "Mark said it's a haunted hayride." She opens her eyes wide with excitement.

Mark? My soaring heart plummets to my feet, like a duck just shot down by some camouflaged jerk and his rifle. Of course Mark would be coming. Mark whose car is parked outside her house almost every day. Mark who walks with her to class. Mark who so obviously wants her, too. And did she say haunted hayride? As in Ol' Gilly's haunted hayride? As in the haunted hayride I swore I'd never participate in again no matter what? I try to recover and not reveal my disappointment, that I actually thought she was asking me out.

I stand there, wondering how the hell I can back out of this now since I have no intention or desire of seeing Mark and Charlotte all chummy chummy together for an enchanted evening. Then out of nowhere, like some kind of devilish imp with supernatural powers, Mark appears.

"Hey, Char-Char, what's up?" He smiles and then barely nods in my direction. "Chunks," he adds. Did he just call her Char-Char? I'm going to puke. My face heats up and I cringe at being called Chunks in front of Char-Char.

"Hey! I was just telling Charlie about the Halloween Hayride. He's coming, too."

"Really?" Mark asks. Charlotte nods, and I shrug my shoulders, pretending not to notice the edge in his voice.

"Yep. Who did you ask?" she says.

Mark stands there for a minute just staring at her,

then at me, then finally says, "Diana."

"Great! She's supersweet," Charlotte says. "Do you know Diana?" she asks looking back at me.

"No." I study Mark who is studying me like I have three heads and someone just told him I'm the king of Spain.

"You'll like her, she's supernice," Charlotte says.

Wait . . . was I getting set up with Diana? Was she some freshman dweeb or something? Was this a joke?

Ahmed comes strutting down the hall a minute later. "Dude, stay away from your locker," he says, fanning the air in front of him. "Smells like ass. I'm not kidding."

"What?" I ask, wondering why of all times, Ahmed has to approach me with a comment like this right now.

"Must be stink bombs, a whole shit load of them, in your locker. It's the worst!" he says, grimacing. "I can still smell it."

"Oh yeah, sorry, Chunks." Mark laughs. I hate the sound of Mark's laughter. It's one of those laughs that's way too loud and forced, like he's having the time of his life, and calls way too much attention to stupid things that don't merit so much attention. My ears pulse.

"Oh, gross," Charlotte whispers with a disgusted look on her face.

"My backpack's in there," I tell them. "And Tanya's not even here today."

"Oh, really?" Mark says. "No way!" He feigns disappointment and then looks directly at me and says, "That sucks."

I meet his glare but say nothing.

It figures. It had been too quiet. In the past month,

there had only been a few run-by crumpled papers chucked at Tanya's head and a couple of crude notes and drawings slipped through the locker vents that I'd thrown out before she found them. I'd been waiting for something bigger (though I'm not sure how you top feces), and here, at last, were the beginnings of Mark's revived machinations. Charlotte gives Mark an annoyed look.

"Sorry," he says, shrugging his shoulders, "really, I had no idea, Chunks. But a guy's gotta do what a guy's gotta do."

Charlotte rolls her eyes. Ahmed looks thoroughly confused.

"Whatever, no big deal," I mutter, wondering how bad it can really be.

"Okay, so we're going to meet here at school on Thursday around eight. But I'll see you before then . . . ," Charlotte says.

"Yeah, right, no problem," I tell her, still trying to figure out how I can get out of this.

"Great. See you tomorrow," she says. "Sorry about your locker." She gives Mark one last meaningful look and turns to leave.

"Wait up, Char-Char," Mark says and follows her. "I'll give you a ride. Good luck, Chunks!" he says, throwing one last evil grin at me. I watch them go, and fight the urge to run after Mark and tackle him to the ground. He was screwing everything up. What the hell just happened?

"What was that all about?" Ahmed asks.

"I'll explain later. Let's go," I say, heading to my fart locker.

"Sorry man, but you're on your own. I'm not going near there again. It's baaaaad . . . bad, bad. You dig? Meet me in the parking lot, but hurry 'cause I have my mom's citizenship thing to go to today," he says, smacking me on the back.

Ahmed is right. It's bad. Real bad. I can smell it way before I get to the hall, and it stops me in my tracks. My stomach lurches as a thousand rotten eggs infiltrate my nostrils and I wonder if I can just ditch my backpack for now. But I have a ton of homework, including an essay due in AP English tomorrow that I'd already started working on. I have to go in. I hate Tanya Bate. If it weren't for her, I wouldn't be dealing with this shit right now. Those bombs were for her, not me. But a flash of Mark's evil grin makes me wonder if that's true.

I race down the empty hall holding my breath. I quickly work the combination, and, of course, it doesn't work the first time. Or the second. Or the third. By the fourth time, I have to breathe through my mouth, which is just as bad because instead of smelling a thousand rotten eggs, it's like I'm eating a thousand rotten eggs. I gag and dry heave. My eyes fill with tears and I can feel my ears burning as I try one last time, but the locker won't open. I give up. It's no use. I run back down the hall trying to hold my breath, but I keep gagging and tasting the toxic smell. Once I'm far enough away, I take a deep breath, but Ahmed was right, the smell gets stuck in your nose. I call him and let him know what's taking so long.

"What are you gonna do?" he asks after I explain I can't get my locker opened.

"I dunno, but I need my essay. I guess I'll go to the office and see if they can get someone to open it, but it's gonna take awhile," I tell him, knowing he has to hurry home, "just go. I'll figure out a way to get home."

"You sure? I'd wait, but . . ."

"Yeah, I know. Don't worry about it. I'll just walk home," I say.

"All right, I'll talk to you later."

I head to the office and tell the front desk attendant that I can't get my locker open, but I leave out the part about the stink bombs because it's too embarrassing. The lady is old, and I have to repeat the whole thing three times before she understands. Then she has to repeat the story to someone else, I guess to the all-knowing High School Oz who makes all the decisions and who finally grants her authority to call the custodian.

After numerous calls to the custodian—and yet another repetition of the situation over the fuzzy static of the all important walkie-talkie used by administration and office personnel—she turns back to me and says, "Go on. Joe will meet you at the locker."

I head back and see Joe, aka the custodian, heading toward me with cutters in his hand. Everyone knows who he is because he's been here forever and is exactly the kind of cantankerous old man who looks like every kid seriously bothers him. But nobody messes with him because even though he's old, he still looks like he wouldn't think twice about beating the crap out of anyone who messed with him. He even has a huge tattoo of a heart and skull on his forearm, which makes me wonder if he's ever killed anyone. I suddenly get to thinking about Joe's life, and I wonder what lead him to be a high school custodian.

"You the boy who can't open your locker?" he calls. I nod and lead him down the hall. He starts complaining of the smell, "Jesus, what the hell is that?" he mutters.

Again, I'm too embarrassed to admit that the smell is coming from my locker.

"Holy shit," he says as we walk closer to the smell. I look over at him a little surprised.

He laughs, gives me a funny look, and says, "You guys go around cursing your asses off and then act surprised when I say it. Watch out." He pushes me out of the way as he whips out the cutters to bust the lock. He clamps down hard only once, and I notice the name "Gina" written across the heart tattoo. I wonder who Gina is.

"Gonna have to buy a new lock," he says. I nod and shrug my shoulders, trying not to breath in the fumes, which is impossible. By now, I feel nauseous.

"There you go." He takes off the lock. I mutter a thanks and open the locker door. The smell explodes out, pushing Joe and me several steps back.

"Holy damn, that smells like toxic shit," he sputters. "Who the hell would do that to you, kid?" he asks.

I can't begin to go into the whole thing about sharing a locker with Tanya, so I just shrug and say, "Some friends playing a joke."

He shakes his head. "Some friends."

He pulls out a dirty handkerchief from his back pocket and covers his nose and mouth with it before stepping forward to take a look. He shakes his head, "Damn stink bombs. Never seen anyone go to the trouble of setting off so many at one time." He shakes his head again.

I look down at the floor, not wanting to make eye contact with this old man who's been around the high school scene long enough to know that nobody who's somebody gets this arsenal of stink bombs put in his locker, no matter who he's sharing it with. If he only knew that there had, in fact, already been shit in my locker this year. He grabs the garbage can in the hall and slides it down to my locker.

"Well, go on. Grab your stuff and get the hell out of here. I'll take care of this," he says.

"I can help," I tell him.

He looks at me for a minute, giving me a sympathetic look before dismissing me with a wave of his hand.

"Go on, kid, it won't take me long," he says.

I grab my corroded backpack, shove a couple of books I need into it, and mumble another quick thanks as I leave.

"So long," he says. I don't reply because something about the way he says it makes me feel sad, and he probably thinks I'm already the biggest wuss on the planet.

When I get to the front of the school, I keep walking. My backpack is ripe with stink, and each step makes me feel sicker. By the time I get home, I'm full-blown nauseous but start the whole process of trying to de-stink my stuff.

I empty out my backpack and wipe down my books, but even after being doused in Lysol, there's still the hint of sulfur on everything. Great, I'll smell like a lingering fart for the next week. I throw my backpack in the washing machine and grab my essay.

When I'm done, Dad calls to check on me and tell me he's definitely going to be late again tonight. When he asks how school was, part of me wants to tell him about the whole locker thing, but I don't because I'm embarrassed about it. I don't want him to know that I've gone through all the trouble of losing weight, and that I'm still pretty much a loser.

After I assure Dad that school couldn't be better and hang up, I get a text from Ahmed:

> Pimp. Mom's thing is almost over.
> B home in 1 hr. Wanna hang?

I text back:

> Cool. C u then.

When I get to Ahmed's, I briefly explain the latest encounter with Charlotte and the Halloween hayride invite. I'm still trying to figure out whether I'm, in fact, being set up with someone, just being invited as a friend, or was quite possibly supposed to go out on some weird group date with Charlotte. Ahmed is jumping up and down on his bed like a crazed chimpanzee, telling me what an idiot I am and that the only possibility is that she digs me.

"Hot diggity, man!" he yells. "You know Janie Haas has been practically knocked off her throne because of Charlotte VanderKleaton, right? Not that Charlotte is prettier, no offense, but she does have that certain . . .

je ne sais quoi," he says, slipping back into smooth Rat Pack mode for a millisecond. "And now," he says as he jumps one last time and lands his ass on the bed, "the chickie is *into* you!" He shakes his head, "It's your year, my man. Definitely your year."

"What about Mark?"

"Screw Mark! Seriously, cat, you have much to learn. If she wasn't into you, she wouldn't have brought it up. And if there was something really going on with her and Mark, that fink would be all over her like a mink on a rich dame. Trust me, the chick digs you. Hey! You ever think about how we're, you know, cats, and girls are chicks and how cats get the little chickies and . . . uh, eat them. Wait, that sounds kind of sick. Hold on . . . do cats *actually* eat chicks? I've never seen one do that. Unless you count Sylvester and Tweety, and technically Tweety was a canary, right? And Sylvester never actually ate him . . . or her. Wait . . . oh shit . . . was Tweety even a girl?" Ahmed is short-circuiting. I swear, sometimes his constant cool cat and spazzo personas are in direct competition with each other.

"Focus," I tell him. "We're talking about Charlotte and me, not Tweety and Sylvester."

"Right, right. Anyway my man, you're a freakin' Casanova. I mean, you got a girl who didn't wait for you to ask her out. *She* asked *you* out!"

"What if she's just being nice?"

"Then you take that nicey-nice and run with it. Make your move, my man!" I shrug, trying not to give the universe the slightest hint that I think this might be the tiniest bit true, because if I do, it'll all blow up in my face.

"Look at you," he says. "You cool, brother. You cooooooool . . ." He makes this slow and smooth gesture with his hand. He gives me a high five, and I suddenly feel like the baddest mothereffer on the planet. I can do this.

CHAPTER SIX

Halloween night doesn't come quick enough. But it does finally come, which also means Mom has been gone for almost two months. She's never been gone for more than six weeks, and that time we knew she was at a cousin's house in Maine for most of it. But this time, something is more off than usual. But then I think it's probably not. This is normal. Any day now she'll just pop right back into our lives, and I'll be pissed that I spent all this time worrying for nothing. I can't do anything about it; I can't make her come back, I can't talk to Dad, and I can't change it, so I put Mom out of my mind and think about Charlotte instead.

Even though I've seen Charlotte a few more times in class since she mentioned the whole hayride thing, I couldn't quite bring myself to ask her, *hey, so, that thing on Thursday, is it a date?* What if it is, and then she realizes what a moron I am?

As I get ready, I have no idea if I'm getting ready for my first date ever, and if so, whether it's with the girl I go to bed dreaming about (and maybe do more than dream about) every night. Or am I just another person in a group simply hanging out together on Halloween? But Ahmed assures me I'm reading way too much into it.

"The chickie digs you!" Ahmed says when I call to ask him if I should really go. "You have to go, man!" So I leave it at that and decide I'm definitely going.

Usually, for Halloween, our house is pretty pimped out. Mom always goes crazy with decorations, though Dad is always the one stuck taking them down. If not, ours would be one of those houses with the ghosts still dangling from our trees in the middle of December. Okay, so that was our house a few years ago, but Dad finally gave in. Mostly because I think he got pissed every time he saw them. Although, I imagine it must have pissed him off even more that he took everything down only to come home from work the next day to Mom's over-the-top Christmas decorations.

Anyway, tonight our house is silent and without the usual blare of Mom's Halloween sound track of wolves howling, witches cackling, and doors squeaking. There are no dangling ghosts, no cardboard headstones, and when the bell rings, I realize too late that neither Dad nor I bought any candy. This is an explanation that doesn't go over too well with the Easter bunny and vampire holding their bags out to me, yelling *trick or treat!* The bunny gives me the finger, and they trample across the dried leaves on our front lawn. I'm surprised Dad hasn't raked them yet. He's usually so anal about that stuff. I close the door and ignore the doorbell the rest of the evening and get ready.

Dad comes home, and a minute later, walks into my room as I spray on some cologne.

"Whoa. Sport, you look great. You and Ahmed hanging out with some 'chickies' this evening?"

"Please never say that again," I say, a little weirded out as he sits down on my bed like he means to hang out here for a while. The last time he came in my room was when he broke the news about sending me to fat camp. I'm hoping he doesn't have any similar news to hit me with tonight.

"You have a date or something?" he asks not being able to keep the genuine surprise out of his voice. I quickly consider my options: tell Dad the truth or just make something up. I resist the impulse to tell him the truth because even though I know Dad would appreciate a father-son moment, I don't think I can explain what tonight is when I don't even know myself, so I think of something quick.

"Nah, just hanging out with some friends."

"Other than Ahmed?" Dad asks with surprise. Can I really blame him? The only person I'd hung out with for the past seven years was Ahmed.

"Yeah," I say casually, "a bunch of guys from my photography class are going. We're just gonna take some pictures at Ol' Gilly's. Then maybe submit them to the yearbook or something." The lies come out so easily. I didn't set out to lie to Dad, but I do, because the truth is too hard to figure out or explain. How can I begin to explain to Dad what Charlotte and I are or aren't, or why the other guy she likes is going, too? And there's no need to verbalize how little game I actually have. Knowing Dad, he'll probably just think I'm in need of another "intervention." And exactly what kind of camp do you send your son to if he has little to no game?

"Wow, that's great!" he says. I can tell he's happy

with the illusion of me actually having friends other than Ahmed.

The doorbell rings again.

"Guess I forgot to buy candy. I have a feeling our house is going to get egged tonight." He sighs.

"Probably." I smooth my hair, take one last look in the mirror, and say, "Gotta go. I'm gonna be late."

"Need a ride?"

"No, I'll walk. It's good exercise." He looks at me even more proudly, and I give him a stupid thumbs-up because I don't know what else to do, and I know I'm not worthy of how he's looking at me right now.

He nods. "Hey, Sport? We're okay, right? You know, just the two of us?" My stomach drops. I know he's referring to more than the weirdness that had been hanging between us since summer. I know he's referring to Mom. This is the closest Dad and I have ever come to really talking about it. But I can't get into this conversation right now. Not before I go on my first maybe-date with the first girl who has ever shown any interest in me.

"Yeah, sure, Dad." I gulp down the little lump of emotion that has risen in my throat. "We're fine. But, uh, I really gotta go. I'll see you later." I say this and go downstairs before Dad can say anything else.

I grab my jacket and camera, which I've started carrying with me in case I see something cool for Killinger's project, and head toward school. The night is cool and I crunch through the dried leaves. I'm glad summer is over because it makes me think of fat camp and how I never want to go back there again. I take lots of deep breaths; the air is cold and helps me wipe out the thought of Dad sitting on my bed by himself. It helps me not to think of the conversation Dad and I would've had if I stayed home tonight. I look up at the sky. There's actually a full moon, so I take out my camera and take a few pictures of it. But Dad's words still linger in my mind. Just the two of us. What did he mean? I think he was asking me if I was okay with things being this way forever. Was I?

I arrive at school, but no one's there yet, so I sit on the bench and wait, forcing myself to think of anything but Mom and Dad.

I've never been to school at night. I've never been to a football game or a basketball game . . . ever. I look around and kick at the floor, thinking I must be the only kid in high school to never have gone to one extracurricular event in his whole high school career. Ahmed goes all the time to these school functions because he says he has to make an appearance for the ladies. But me? No way. I can't get into a sports game because who am I rooting for? Kids who don't give two shits about me? Kids who have whispered behind my back for the last three years every time I had to squeeze out of a desk and slosh up the aisle to get a paper from some stupid teacher who obviously doesn't understand what it is like to have thirty pairs of eyes stare at your fat ripples? I couldn't be part of it. I look toward the hall where my locker is, and Tanya's gross face pops into my head. I wonder if that's how she feels, too. Does that mean I'm like her?

No, we're nothing alike because Tanya Bate is at

home reciting lines to the latest *Lord of the Rings* movie and I'm here. This is what life is like when you're normal, when you're one of them.

I look at my watch. It's fifteen minutes past the time we were supposed to meet. Where are they? Another five minutes tick by. There's no way I could have possibly gotten the wrong night. Kids with costumes had rung my doorbell. It was definitely Halloween. Did I get the wrong time? A sinking feeling suddenly comes over me; this is a joke. My God, they've pulled the ultimate loser prank. Ask the prettiest girl in school to ask out the fat kid—or formerly fat kid—and see if he shows up. I look around to see if anyone is spying on me. My chest tightens.

Suddenly, a whooping sound and girls' laughter comes from somewhere deep in the maze that is our school. *Oh no.* It gets louder and I easily make out Charlotte's voice, having memorized every pitch and timber of it. Soon five figures emerge—Charlotte, Mark, Danny with his on-again/off-again girlfriend, Trisha, who is loud and obnoxious and a little scary, and another girl wearing a lot of makeup and really tight clothes who I assume must be Diana, but . . . they're not pointing at me or saying *he fell for it, oh my God, he actually fell for it!* I'm flooded with relief, kind of.

"Hey, Chunks!" Mark's loud voice calls out. Instantly, my back gets hot and prickly and my face flushes.

"What's up?" I say, still preparing myself in case this is a joke. I feel like punching Mark every time he calls me that in front of Charlotte.

"What the hell are you doing?" he asks. "We've been

waiting in the parking lot for the last fifteen minutes for your sorry ass."

Immediately I realize my mistake. Of course they would be waiting for me in the parking lot—the *student* parking lot. Because they (or at least Mark) have cars, but I, the formerly fat but ever constant loser, did not have a car.

"Just thought I'd check the place out," I tell them, feigning a coolness I definitely did not feel. I look at Charlotte. She looks great. She smiles at me, whispers a soft hey, and waves as the light from the moon catches her eyes at just the right angle, making them look extra sparkly. She stands next to me. Mark watches her and slips his arm around Diana.

"So, listen, I know you share a locker with Tanya Bate," he says, "so sorry about the stink bombs." He gives me a hard look. I know he's really not because then he looks at Charlotte for approval. "Anyway, we're going to lay off the locker," he says and looks over at her again. Diana watches the exchange, and her eyes narrow.

"But," Mark continues, "you know, we have to do something else and coming up with just the right thing has really tested my creativity. I mean most things just seem, so . . . so . . ." He thinks a moment. "Typical," he says finally. "But fear not, Mark Delancey does not back down from a challenge." Diana looks up at him a little too adoringly. Danny's face is bright with anticipation. And I feel like telling him to just lay off Tanya altogether. It really pisses me off that Mark feels it's his duty to torment people. Why can't he just leave her alone?

"It took some time, but I think I've come up with a golden plan. However, it's up to you to execute." Damn. Whatever is coming is not good. Whatever is coming is bigger than the time they sprinkled itching powder on her head, and five minutes into class she was scratching like crazy and the teacher had to send her to the clinic. It's bigger than the time they grabbed the sports bottle she used to carry to every class and spit in it so that when she took a drink and it was clogged, she tried harder. This apparently forced the slimy loogie through the nozzle and into her mouth, at which point she spit the water out all over herself and everyone laughed.

They look at me expectantly. I don't want any part of what he's about to tell me. Observing Tanya's fucked-up life is one thing, but actually fucking it up is completely different. Something in my gut tells me, *don't do it*. But I also know I can't tell him no.

"How?" I ask as regret and concession hit me as soon as the word leaves my mouth.

Mark narrows his eyes and sizes me up, "I don't know . . . think you can handle it?"

I shrug and look over at Charlotte. She looks over at Mark. Diana looks over at Mark. Mark looks back at me and takes something out of his pocket. "With a little of this," he says, holding out a small baggie with what looks like dried-up sticks and leaves.

"What?" I ask.

"Whaddya mean what? Grisner . . . where have you been living, in a freakin' hobbit hole with Tanya Bate? It's weed, dumbass."

I can feel my face get hot.

"Oh . . ." Stupid, stupid. "I couldn't see it," I say. I wasn't fooling Mark.

"Right." He snickers. "Whatever. Anyway, the plan is to get that dweeb freakin' stoned off her ass during school, so we can all see her high as hell. It's freakin' perfect!" He laughs that miserably loud laugh I can't stand.

"High as hell?" I mutter. "That doesn't make sense." I have no idea why I said that and instantly regret it.

"Oh my God, Chunks," he says, forcing another laugh that gets louder and louder. "What are you, a damn English teacher? High as hell," he mocks, using this ridiculously exaggerated geek voice. "That doesn't make sense. That's not technically correct. Geez, man, lighten up!"

Danny laughs too, and Trisha shakes her head and rolls her eyes, not because she has any compassion for me but because she doesn't like Mark that much, which is why, apparently, Danny's and her relationship is always on again/off again.

"Stop," Charlotte says to him, smacking him lightly on his chest. Mark rubs his chest where she touched him.

"But how are you going to get her to smoke it?" I ask finally, trying to cover up my last mess up.

Mark shakes his head and laughs again. "Oh my God, Grisner, you're killing me. She's not gonna smoke it—she's gonna eat it. All I gotta do is add a little of this to some brownie mix and then," he pauses for dramatic effect, *"you're gonna get her to eat one."*

Crap.

"Me?" My voice sounds squeaky.

"Yes, you," Mark says. I feel like an idiot.

"But . . ."

"But, what? I mean, you guys do share a locker, right? You're practically BFFs." He grins. Asshole. "Anyway, she's definitely not going to eat anything we give her. Come on. It'll be funny, dude!"

Charlotte reaches for my hand, and even though it's sweaty, she holds it. "Ordinarily, I would not approve of such things," she explains, "but . . . it *is* pretty funny."

I know if I don't agree soon, it's all over. They'll think I'm a wuss or a Goody Two-Shoes or something. Or worse, I could lose Charlotte. I look at her, who despite the fact thinks this is a good idea, she still looks as pretty and sweet as ever.

"Okay," I say, ignoring the sudden lurch in my stomach. Mark looks suspicious and slightly disappointed that I actually accepted the challenge, but the rest of them laugh as we head to the parking lot.

• • •

The rest of the night almost makes me forget the pact I just made with the devil's offspring. Ol' Gilly Farms had put on this Halloween Hayride for as long as I could remember. Ahmed and I convinced our parents to let us go by ourselves when we were in the sixth grade, and I had been scared out of my mind. The image of corpses and limbless people dripping with blood stayed with me for weeks afterward. Not to mention how some high school kid had yelled, "Hey, look at the little fat kid!" to his group of friends when one of the chainsaw creeps jumped on and hovered over me, and I closed my eyes and started grabbing at anyone near me for protection—which just happened to be this tiny girl who couldn't weigh more than ninety-five pounds and couldn't shield one of my legs, much less the rest of me. They laughed as I cowered behind her and she screamed, "Ewww . . . you smell like BO!" while trying to push my sweaty self away. I had in fact forgotten to put on deodorant that night and was sweating like a pig. Those words stayed with me longer than the creepy images, and I swore I would never return to Ol' Gilly's.

But tonight, Charlotte is at my side, holding my hand, grabbing my arm, throwing herself at *me* for protection, and I had put on extra deodorant this time. Eerie music plays as we travel along the trail, along with screams, cackles, and pleas for help from victims who sound like they're being hacked to pieces somewhere out in the forest surrounding the trail.

Mark and Danny ask the chainsaw creeps that jump on if they know where their mamas had been last night. The crowd laughs at Mark and Danny's obnoxiousness, especially some loud college guys who think the two are the best damn thing since beer bongs. I kind of laugh too, but really, it's like I'm not there at all. It's like I have cotton stuffed in my ears, like I am caught in a dream, because nothing else exists—not mummies or headless French maids, not Tanya Bate and the pot-brownie prank, not Danny or Trish or Diana or Mark—who keeps looking at me like he wants to kill me each time Charlotte holds on to me. The only thing I can focus on is Charlotte's body next to mine, the way her hands feel clutching me closer to her. And how I know

I'll never forget any of it.

After the hayride, we grab something to eat at a late night joint I've never been to. I order like everyone else because I don't want to draw any attention to what I'm eating. Still, I worry the whole time that Mark is going to make some kind of smart remark about how fat I used to be, but he doesn't and we finally head home. Mark makes a point about bringing up the fact that I don't own a car when he realizes why I wasn't in the parking lot waiting for them.

"Mommy still driving you around?" he says, looking at me in the rearview mirror. The mention of my mom makes my stomach flip.

"Oh, shut up," Charlotte says, but she does it in this sweet way that doesn't sound mean at all. Diana is reapplying lipstick and eyes Charlotte in the mirror. Charlotte smiles at her.

"Oh come on, I'm just joking. You know I'm just joking, don't you, Chunks?" Mark says.

"Yeah, of course," I lie as we keep driving.

The whole drop-off thing is a mess when it becomes obvious to everyone that Mark is trying everything in his power to make Charlotte's stop the last one. Like it makes sense to pass our neighborhood and then drop everyone else off first when it would be easier to drop Charlotte and me off first. Or that he's taking this circuitous route simply because he loves driving at night. It's all too clear that Mark has a serious thing for Charlotte, especially to Diana who, after fumbling for her keys for a full three minutes on the sidewalk, finally gets the clue that Mark won't bother getting out of the car, and she stomps up to her house. He calls out, "later," and speeds off before she gets to her front door. We drop off Trish and Danny next, and finally, pull up to my house where, to Mark's dismay, Charlotte gets out too.

"Where you going?" Mark asks her, not able to hide the desperation in his voice. "Don't you want me to drop you off?"

"No, that's okay. Charlie will walk me home, right, Charlie?" I nod. Of course I would walk her home. I would walk anywhere for Charlotte.

"Come on, Char-Char, that makes no sense. Just let me drop you off at home," Mark says.

"I'm fine. Just go ahead," Charlotte answers.

She slams the door shut and leans down onto the passenger side window, "I'll see you tomorrow, okay?" she says. I stand on the curb, my hands in my pockets, strangely feeling like I shouldn't be here. Charlotte mumbles something else, and a minute later, Mark screeches away from the curb and speeds down the street. Charlotte watches for a minute and then turns to me.

"What was that all about?" I ask.

"Oh, he's always mad about something," Charlotte says. We start walking toward her house. A couple of straggling trick-or-treaters are still making the rounds but soon give up when it looks like nobody is answering their doors.

"So, that was fun tonight," she says. Her skin looks pale and surreal by the moonlight. "Did you have fun?"

I nod. "Yeah, lots."

"Don't worry about Mark. That's just the way he is

to everyone. Underneath he's a pretty cool guy."

"Right."

"No, really, he is," she insists. I shrug my shoulders and look down at the sidewalk wishing she weren't talking about Mark to me.

"You know, you don't *have* to do that thing to Tanya."

A wave of relief floods over me. She doesn't really expect me to do this. Maybe she just said it was a good idea because she was around Mark.

"But," she says with a shrug, "it would be kind of funny."

Damn.

"Yeah." I force a smile. "I mean, I'll try, but I don't know if she'll actually go for it, you know?"

"She will. You're such a nice guy, and she'll never guess what you're up to."

"Maybe," I say as we round the corner leading to her house.

"Definitely," she says and links her arm through mine the rest of the way.

The more we walk, the more my heart beats faster and my breathing comes in short gasps. I wonder if Charlotte expects me to kiss her. Part of me wishes that Mark had just dropped her off at her house because now I'm plagued with this whole kissing conundrum. Holy shit. I don't even know how to kiss. I've never kissed a girl before in my life. This is not good—I mean it's wonderful . . . but also not good. Even though I want to kiss her, I'm scared as hell.

"Aren't you?' she says. I look over at her and realize I've been so worried about a possible kiss that I haven't paid attention to anything she's just said.

"Huh?" I say.

"I said," she says and gives me a small nudge, "I'm glad we ended up as partners in drama."

"Yeah, totally." We slow to a stop in front of her house.

"Well, here we are. . . ." She sighs and lets go of my arm. My legs feel like two globs of Jell-O.

"Yeah." I take a deep breath. "Here we are." Silence. I look up at the moon because I feel weird looking straight at her.

"You're a really nice guy, Charlie," she says. "I feel like, I don't know, like . . . you're deeper than most guys." She looks over at me and then shakes her head. "That was stupid. Oh my God, I'm so stupid sometimes." And I don't know how I know, but I know this is it. This is my chance to kiss her, to make happen what I've been hoping for all summer. And before I lose my nerve or she can say anything else, I lean toward her. I watch her eyes close a second before I close mine and then Charlotte VanderKleaton's lips touch mine. It's a soft lingering kiss that makes my whole body feel weak. She tastes like strawberries, and her mouth is warm. It's the greatest thing I've ever felt.

I touch my hand to my lips as she pulls back and smiles. She turns and runs up to her door, and for a minute, I think I've seriously screwed up. But then she turns back, smiles at me, and calls out, "Good night, Charlie," in the best possible way.

I can't say anything, and then she's gone.

After I recover from the shock, I run home and start laughing out loud from the extreme giddiness. Charlotte

VanderKleaton likes me. I can still feel her lips, the remnants of her strawberry lips. My head and chest are flooded with feelings of awesomeness as I walk the rest of the way home. I did it. I kissed her. I kissed Charlotte VanderKleaton!

As I get closer to my house, I try to calm down. Not that Dad will get up and drill me about where I was, but I'd rather not have to explain why I didn't tell him about Charlotte in the first place. If I tell him, Dad might ask me to bring her over, which means I'd be opening her up to my screwy world. So there's no reason to tell any one about each other. I stop at the corner and take some deep breaths. Once my breathing becomes normal, I walk the rest of the way.

My house is dark and quiet. I look at my watch. 12:45 a.m. I insert the key into the door and sneak in quietly.

I hear a low murmur coming from Dad's office. I look over; his room is dark, but there it is, the low murmur again. I inch toward the door and listen. "Yeah, I love you, too." Is he talking to Mom? Has she finally called? Maybe she's ready to come home. She does that sometimes, calls before coming home. Maybe she's just checking if it's okay, to see if we're mad at her because she's been gone so long.

But after a minute, I realize something's not right. Dad's voice sounds different. It's light. It's happy. It's so unlike any other time he's ever talked to Mom. My heart pounds furiously because suddenly I know it's not Mom on the other end of the line.

The information connects instantly, and my brain starts telling me to get the hell out of here before he hears me. But my body stays stuck in place. I can't believe what I'm hearing. Dad is laughing and making promises to see her soon.

I step back from the door, but bump into the small table in the corner. It makes the slightest noise that suddenly halts the murmuring. I try to think quickly.

"Charlie?" he calls from the other side of the door. Shit. I grab the handle of the front door and open it noisily.

"Charlie?" Dad swings open his office door just as I slam the front door shut and pretend to have just gotten home.

"Hey, Dad. Sorry, I didn't mean to slam it."

"You . . . you just getting in?" he asks.

"Yeah, sorry, I know I'm a little late, but it just worked out better for Tom to drop everyone else off first." The fake name comes to me easily.

"Oh, right . . ." He rubs the back of his neck. "I didn't hear a car," he says.

"Really?" I swallow hard, and just as quickly as it comes to me, the lie floats out of my mouth. "I'm surprised. Tom's car is an old clunker." I bounce the focus back on to him and try to keep my voice as light as possible. "You must have been pretty focused on what you were doing. Work keeping you up late?"

And there it is. He directs his gaze to the floor, shrugs his shoulders, and stuffs his hands into his pockets. His face looks slightly flushed as he shifts his weight uncomfortably.

"Yeah, just finishing up."

"Oh, okay. Well, I better get to bed. I'm pretty

tired," I tell him.

"Yeah, yeah, me too," he says, "just one last e-mail to send." I head to my room, refusing to look back at him.

"Sport?" he calls as I reach the top of the stairs. I stop and turn around halfway. "Are you all right?"

I clear my throat. "Yeah," I say, louder than I mean to.

"Okay then, good night," he calls out just as I make it to my room.

I close the door and lie down without bothering to change my clothes. *Dad is cheating on Mom.* It seems incredibly unreal. It's . . . I can't even imagine Dad talking to another woman, putting us completely out of his mind like that. I can't imagine him anywhere but here. Was he happy away from us? Did he wish he could take off and never come back? Or is this what he meant by "just the two of us?"—like if Mom never came back?

And then it hits me. Mom must have found out. This is why she's gone. This is why he sent me to fat camp. Not because he cares about me, not because he knows how hard things are for a fatty, but because he was trying to get rid of me and do whatever the hell he wanted with some other woman. All this time, he let me think it was me. He let me think my weight was the big stress between him and Mom, but it wasn't me. It was them and how freakin' selfish they are. And this is why Dad kept asking if I was okay. This is why he gave me a hundred fucking dollars for my birthday because of his guilt.

And now I'm in all of this alone. The only person who I thought got it, who I thought I might be able to count on, has left me too.

PART TWO
EXPOSURE

CHAPTER SEVEN

Here's what I know:
Dad isn't who I thought he was.
Mom is who she's always been.
I am not who I want to be (still).
This is who we are.
Here's what I don't know:
If this is who we'll always be.

• • •

"Hey, Sport," Dad says to me the next morning. I'm about to bolt and wait outside for Ahmed when he hits me with, "What do you know about these video cameras that attach to your computer? I have to get one for my conference calls."

I can't believe it. I can't believe that he actually has the nerve to say it so casually. I look over at him, and just like I figured, he's not looking back at me. He's too busy texting on his BlackBerry, and it's probably to her, even as he stands in the same room as me.

"Nothing. I don't know anything about them," I say as his phone buzzes with an incoming message. He looks down at it and smiles.

"Eh, all right. I guess I'll just ask the guy at the store." His teeth seem whiter than usual. It pisses me off and quickens the realization that Dad is a lying phony.

His hair is neatly combed back; his shirt, tie, and slacks are crisp and perfectly pressed. He irons everything himself because he doesn't think the drycleaners do a good enough job. The way he's so immaculately groomed is extremely irritating, and I have to fight the urge not to tell him to go to hell. But I don't want him to know that I know because what will happen when he doesn't have to hide it anymore? He takes a sip of his coffee and looks up at the ceiling before looking over at me.

"You okay, Sport?" His brow furrows.

"Yeah, fine, just tired," I mumble.

"Me, too." He sighs. It's déjà vu and I wonder if this is all Dad and I will ever say to each other. He seems like he wants to say more, but he doesn't. We pretend not to notice the awkward silence that fills the air, the weirdness that has come back tenfold from the summer, until finally, Dad looks at his watch.

"Hey, listen, Sport. I gotta fly outta town to Chicago for a couple of days. I'm heading straight to the airport now. It's last minute, but," he pauses, "anyway, you think you'll be okay on your own for a few days?"

My stomach drops. He goes on to overexplain why he has to go, giving too many details about some emergency finance meeting.

"Yeah, I'll be fine." I cut him off because I'll lose it if he tells me another damn lie.

This is too much for me to deal with. It's not just his lying and sneaking around that makes the whole situation unbearable. It's something else, something that goes much deeper. It's like a seriously screwed-up sense of understanding. Because I get it. I know why he's doing this. And I hate that I get it.

But he's dead wrong if he thinks I'm going to be his little accomplice. Freaking portable video cameras and a sudden out-of-town meeting . . . on a Friday? He obviously thinks I'm an idiot who can't figure shit out.

"You sure you'll be all right?" he asks. A shadow passes over his face, and I think that maybe if I say no, he might stay. But it doesn't matter. He's already decided to go.

I nod.

"I'll call and check up," he says as he heads to the door, his carry-on and briefcase propped up next to it. His stupid shoes click on the tiled kitchen floor as he walks to the back door. He's almost outside when the words come out of me.

"Hey, Dad?"

"Yeah, Sport?" his head pops back into the kitchen.

"Sorry you have to figure it out on your own," I say. His smile disappears. He looks back at me, and his eyes flicker with a sudden understanding.

"Oh. You mean the video camera? Yeah, don't worry about it, Sport." He looks at me funny, and stops for a minute like he's going to say something.

"All right, well, talk to you soon," he says and shuts the door behind him.

I drink the rest of my orange juice in silence, thinking about how I'm sitting in this kitchen alone. I think about how my mom is God knows where. How my dad is heading to God knows where. And I'm stuck here—all by myself.

• • •

School sucks all day. I can't think of anything except Dad and the mystery woman he was talking to. The teachers drone on, and more than once I have to ask someone what we're doing. By the time photography comes around I'm tired of thinking and put my head on the table waiting for class to start.

Right now I want to stop time; stop the harsh squeak of someone's sneakers as they hurry in, the scrape of chairs being pulled out and pushed back in, the layers of voices and conversations that fill the room. When I was younger, I used to watch some reruns of a TV show about a girl who could stop time just by touching the tips of her index fingers together. I keep my head pressed on the cold table, close my eyes, and slowly bring my fingers together.

The bell rings.

Mr. Killinger's voice fills the room, slowly snuffing out the swell of conversation until only he is speaking.

"All right, people. You have exactly four weeks to finish your collections," he says, "then, that first week in December, we will have judging here at school. The panel of judges will include my mentor, Dr. Hoyt, your principal, and other Rennington College and Kennedy High faculty. They will choose the winning collection that, in turn, will be displayed the following week at Rennington's annual fine arts show." He smiles. "It's a big deal guys. Pretty cool stuff."

I think of how I haven't worked on this yet, and probably should. Why the hell haven't I when taking pictures is the only thing I'm good at? But thinking of all that starts crowding my head. And I wish I could will myself to think of nothing, but when you try to think of nothing, you end up thinking of everything, especially of how shitty your Dad is.

"So, that translates to . . . you better be working on it! Seriously, I want some good stuff. Remember, you want enough time to compose your artist's statement explaining your photographs. You should include what the photos represent and how they fit together as a collection. Some of you are probably already at that stage, or at least have an idea of what to write." *I mean he was married. Is married. Even if Mom is never around. . . .*

People around me open their books, start working on artist's statements, and talk to each other about their collections. Some have even brought in their pictures and begin showing them to others. I open my notebook and stare at a blank page. Despite his sending me to fat camp, I had always thought of Dad as the good guy and Mom as the bad guy. But maybe I had it wrong all this time. Maybe Dad was bad and Mom was good, but then, why would she abandon us like she always does? My head hurts. I can't think about this anymore but I can't stop. Then suddenly Mr. Killinger comes up behind me.

"Having trouble?" he asks. I shrug my shoulders. "Need help?" I don't answer him.

"Have you started thinking about your collection yet?" he continues.

No, I haven't thought about it because my dad is having an affair, and my mom can't stand to be around me. It won't be long before Charlotte sees how screwed up I am, and she'll eventually disappear too. And there's no escaping any of this. . . .

I shrug again and focus on the blank page in front of me because I can't look him in the eye. He stays silent for a minute, but he's still standing next to me.

"Hey . . . why don't you hang out for a while after class, okay?" I don't say anything, but he waits. I nod and he finally walks away. I put my head down and close my eyes for the rest of the class.

The bell rings. Everyone packs up their stuff and starts heading out.

"Wanna talk about it?" Mr. Killinger comes over to my table once the last person has left the room. He pulls out a chair and sits next to me. I'm glad he's not facing me. He's being nice, but I wish he'd leave me alone. Things are so much easier when you're big and fat and everyone pretends you don't exist. I keep my head bowed.

"Charlie . . . I can tell something's wrong. I know you don't want the lame lecture teachers usually give, but . . ." He chooses his words. "You can talk to me. Sometimes, it helps to just get it out."

I wish I could open my mouth and let everything come out. But it feels glued shut.

"Is it something here at school?" he asks. I shake my head no.

"Home?" The word is depressing. I don't say anything.

"Okay . . . is it your parents?" I nod.

"It's all right, Charlie, you can talk about it." I wish

I could. I really do. But I'm not going to.

"Are they on your case about something?" Silence fills the air and it makes me hot and uncomfortable. I wish I could tell him something, anything, just to get this over with, if only to fill the silence. I clear my throat.

"It's . . ." My voice sounds hoarse. I clear my throat and try again. "It's . . . I just don't get them," I tell him finally, amazed at how much effort it takes to just say that. I don't know how else to sum it all up. My mouth refuses to elaborate. But my brain keeps spinning the truth. *Mom is crazy and gone all the time, and Dad is sleeping with some other woman in Chicago. Mom is crazy and gone all the time, and Dad is sleeping with some other woman in Chicago. . . .*

"Oh," he says, "it must be pretty bad." I just shrug in response.

"Is there a lot of yelling?" he asks. No, just silence. No one is ever home. But I just nod again.

"Anything more than yelling . . . ?" I look over at him for the first time since we started talking. He looks genuinely concerned.

I still don't know how to answer. Yes, it's so much more than yelling, but . . .

"Anything . . . any . . . physical altercations?" he asks.

I shake my head, no. We're very good at hurting each other without any altercations, without being in the same room, without being in the same house.

"Well . . . ," his voice trails off. "Listen, Charlie, I understand what it's like living in a house where there's a lot of . . . tension," he says. "It's hard. A lot harder than people think."

"Yeah," I croak, wishing so bad I could tell him the rest; wishing the words in my head would actually come out of my mouth. But they don't, and we sit there again in silence. He doesn't tell me it will get better. He doesn't tell me not to worry. He tells me it sucks and sometimes kids get a raw deal. It's not fair but it's true, and if I need to talk to someone, he'll listen.

"Here." He reaches in his pocket and pulls out his wallet. He slips a business card out and hands it to me.

"Give me a call whenever. I'm serious," he says. "Anytime."

The card has an image of a vintage looking camera in the corner, and in the middle there's a phone number and an e-mail address along with:

Luka Killinger

Freelance Photographer

"Luka?" It's weird when you learn a teacher's first name, especially when it's a name like Luka.

"Oh, it gets much worse. Luka Sue, actually," he says. I turn to see how gullible he thinks I am.

"No way," I tell him. Who the hell names a boy Sue? Luka Sue?

He still has his wallet in his hand, so he digs out his driver's license and drops it on the table. Luka Soo Killinger.

"Oh, but it's Soo." I say even though I've never heard the name Soo. I kind of laugh and shake my head.

"Doesn't matter how you spell it. It's still Sue," he says. He takes back his license and tucks it into his wallet.

"Actually, both are names of songs. My mom was obsessed with Johnny Cash. One of his songs was about a boy named Sue, S-U-E, but, well, anyway, guess you could say she had a sense of humor and was a bit of a free spirit. I'm just glad it's not my first name, you know?"

I nod and look down at my hands. Silence.

"Charlie," he says, "parents . . . they're never perfect and lots of times are very different from who we think they are or who we want them to be."

I nod and stare at the card in my hand. He's getting too close to the truth. The silence hangs in the air. I feel like I'm going to suffocate.

"Harrison," I say finally.

He looks at me funny.

"My middle name," I tell him. "Charles Harrison Grisner."

"I would have killed for a name like that," he says. I try to laugh and it helps.

I sit there for another minute. I can tell he's just giving me time, but I'm ready to go.

"Well, I guess I better go to lunch," I say because I don't know how to end this weird TV-sitcom moment. I get up to leave.

"Okay. But listen . . . ," he says, "anytime, all right?" I look over at him, and I can tell he means it. He's not just playing the part of the concerned teacher.

"Yeah, okay . . . thanks." I put the card in my back pocket and make a mental note to put it somewhere safe once I get home. I grab my backpack.

"See you later . . . Sue," I say as I leave.

"Later, Harrison," he calls out.

• • •

Sixth period drama rolls around and I watch the door, hoping she will be in class. If Charlotte's not in class today, I'm just going to put my head down and hope the world ends. The door opens, and she comes in and slides into her seat next to me.

"Hey," she says with a sweet smile. Just having her this close makes everything else go away. "I looked for you at lunch. . . ."

Really? She was looking for me?

"Oh, sorry, teacher kept me after class."

"Bummer," she says, and then looks at me with a coy shyness I'm sure she doesn't actually feel. "So . . . ," she continues, dragging out the word, "last night was fun."

I smile, suddenly remembering last night. I laugh nervously as a thousand butterflies flap like mad in my stomach.

When the night comes flooding back, I need a glass of water. I haven't even had a chance to relive the kiss since it happened—how her lips felt and the warmth of her mouth. The butterflies multiply to a trillion.

"Yeah. Very, uh, wow," I say. I'm a bumbling idiot. "I mean, very cool," I manage, finally.

"We should do it again sometime," she says, "like, maybe tonight?"

I swallow hard, laugh for no reason, and nod. Her eyes flicker, satisfied with my reaction. The bell rings. The last of the presentations start, and she sits back and flashes a smile every time I look her way. When the bell rings ending class, she asks me to come over to her house to watch a movie tonight. Her house, just the two of us—no Mark, no Danny, no annoying other girls. Just us. Charlotte and Charlie. And even though I start warning myself that this is too good to be true, I agree and thank God for creating Charlotte VanderKleaton. I'm thankful she's here because if I didn't have her to look forward to, I wouldn't have anything else. If I've found my way to Charlotte's heart, I want to bury myself there forever, even if she doesn't remember or notice I'm there. I don't mind, just as long as she lets me stay.

Ahmed drops me off at home, and I head inside trying to focus on what happened after drama. I make a dash for the stairs, still fantasizing about tonight. Would we kiss again—or maybe more? The thought makes me feel like laughing, screaming, and jumping. It's all busting to get out, so I start yelling and dancing around because I can't help it.

The phone rings and I answer it slightly out of breath from some improv moves that would thoroughly impress Ahmed.

"Hello?" There's no answer on the other end, and for a minute I wonder if it could possibly be Charlotte joking around. But then I remember she doesn't have my home number.

"Hello?" The silence on the other end is broken by some muffled noise. I think I hear a voice, but I'm not sure.

"*Hello?*" No response.

If I were normal—if my life was normal—I would hang up. But because I'm me, I hang on to the phone and wait. I know exactly who it is.

"Mom? Mom, say something, it's Charlie," I say, though, of course, she knows it's me. "Mom . . . where are you?" She still says nothing. "We're okay. How are you?" Still no answer and I start to feel helpless. Mom's done this before, and eventually she says something. "Are you coming back soon? We miss you." And even though I say it, it doesn't sound genuine, even to me. "Mom? Mom?" No answer. I stay on the phone for another couple of minutes trying to get her to say something, but she doesn't, and I wonder how long I should stand here with the receiver to my ear, talking to myself. When she doesn't respond, I start getting mad. I don't have time to do this.

"Mom, I want to talk to you but I have to go. Just . . ." I sigh and curse myself for being such a shitty son. "Just take care of yourself and come home, Mom, okay? Come home." No answer. I hang up and immediately feel guilty. Why couldn't I just talk to her for another minute? Maybe she was going to say something the second right before I hung up. Maybe she was thinking of coming back and now she wouldn't. And it would be because of me.

I grab my backpack and head upstairs. Maybe it's because I just talked to her, but when I pass Mom and Dad's bedroom, my mind plays tricks on me and I swear I see some blurry figure standing near Mom's easel set up near their window. I stop dead in my tracks and go back to look, but nothing's there. I go in and look around, but still nothing.

I look at the canvas still on the easel and the brushes with dried-up paint that no one bothered to clean up. I haven't been in my parent's bedroom since Mom left, which is why I haven't seen her latest painting. It's different than what she usually paints. The usual flowers, vases, and fruits are nowhere to be found in the grayish brown, black, and blue swirls. I stare at it. The streaks and swirls outline a head and face if you look hard and long enough, then there are two dark smudges where the eyes should be. No nose. No mouth. Instead there are ribbons of murky gray that explode all around the face, which snake around the neck. The ribbons look like they're strangling whoever the person in the painting is supposed to be, which can only be Mom. This was a painting of herself. This is how Mom feels. I stare at it for a minute. I should've stayed on the phone longer. When I leave their room those swirls of gray, black, and blue stay in my head, tightening around Mom's neck.

I hang around doing nothing, trying not to think about where Dad is or what he's doing while I'm here, answering Mom's weird phone calls and staring at her messed-up paintings. I hide in my room and then wander around the house. I hate that he's not here because it means that I'm not enough and that Dad doesn't care enough to stick around either.

I look in the fridge and can tell that at some point before he left, Dad went shopping and stocked up on healthy foods. There's fruit and lettuce and fat-free dressing, but the last thing I feel like doing is fixing myself some stupid low-cal meal, slapping a smile on my face, and pretending it's the most delicious thing I've ever eaten. I order a pizza instead, and when it arrives, I tell myself I'm only going to eat one slice. But I don't and end up eating two. And then since I didn't stick to my original plan, I grab a third. And then I've fucked up so bad already, I eat two more, which means there's only one slice left which looks pathetic. It only reminds me how many I already ate, so I stuff it in my mouth. It doesn't even taste good, but I eat it anyway because I don't want to look at that slice all by itself in the cardboard box.

I stare at the empty box and feel even worse.

I go to the kitchen and open the fridge for something to drink, but there's only water, which at this point seems about as stupid as a diet soda. I know I should stop, but I can't. Fuck it.

I run down to the basement where I know Mom always keeps a few liters of soda. Grape, Orange, or Cola. I can't decide. It's been so long since I felt the fizzy comfort of any of them. I open them and take a big swig of each. My stomach feels like I'm going to explode, and just when I am, a huge belch hisses right out of me. Pieces of pizza come up with it, and I start to gag. I think of all the food sitting in my stomach, and I can picture Fat Camp Ramona with frosting around her mouth when I had come up on her hiding in the woods. She was eating cupcakes when we were all supposed to be on a nature hike. It was pathetic. Imagine what I must look like now. The soda bubbles up like Alka-Seltzer, and it makes the pizza become an effervescent trail of chunks coming up my throat.

I run to the basement bathroom and make it just in time. It all comes up, clumps of food kerplunk in the toilet with such a thud that the water splashes up on my face, making me gag even more so that the rest of it all comes up. I kneel there, the pizza in the toilet and watery grossness dripping from my nose. I'm spent, exhausted, disgusted, but I feel empty. I feel like all those words I hold in and stuff down came up, too, and are swirling around in the bowl with the rest of it. I can just flush all 'of it down and get rid of it. Like it never existed. Like nothing happened.

CHAPTER EIGHT

I change my shirt, brush my teeth, wash my face, and head to Charlotte's. Even though this is monumental and very likely the best thing to happen to me in my whole life since our kiss, I feel like crap. All I can think of is that stupid phone call and painting. Why did she have to call today, right at that moment? Why couldn't she wait until tomorrow so I could at least enjoy tonight? Why couldn't Dad be there to answer it instead of me? But now, I won't be able to enjoy tonight because all I can think about is Mom and how she could be dead. Maybe she called me as she was dying and that's why she didn't talk to me. Maybe the blurry figure I thought I saw in her room was her ghost. Maybe Mom is dead right now while I'm on my way to Charlotte's house, and Dad is somewhere with some other woman. What if Mom is looking down at us right now and thinking how glad she is to be dead and far away from the worst husband and son?

I get to Charlotte's house, and I'm not even sure how I got there so fast. When she answers the door and says hey the same way she always does in drama, my thoughts of Mom still don't go away. I mumble hi and smile and meet her mother who is in the kitchen and looks like an older version of Charlotte. She's baking cookies—actually baking cookies—and looks really dressed up like she just got home from work. She flashes me a big red lipsticky smile and says, "Nice to meet you, Charlie. Hope you like cookies. They're made with the best Belgian chocolate!" She seems very cheery and immediately makes me think of chefs on cooking shows and how they talk into the camera. I nod because I don't know what to say, and she flashes me another huge smile.

Then her smile suddenly fades when she turns her attention to Charlotte. "Oh honey, why don't you pull your hair back? I can't stand seeing it in your face that way," she says, shaking her head.

"It's fine, Mom," Charlotte says with a sigh.

Her mom studies Charlotte, then begins scooping little balls of dough on a baking tray with a mini ice-cream scooper. "It looks neater pulled back, Charlotte. I always say that but you never listen." She looks over at me. "Charlotte here can be a bit of a slob." She winks at me. I feel weird. I didn't see anything wrong with Charlotte's hair, so I don't say anything.

"Mom, I swear, why can't you just—"

"Charlotte," her mom says with an edge in her voice, "not in front of your guest." Then she looks at me again and asks, "Don't you think she should show off her pretty face, Charlie?"

I don't know what to say and luckily I don't have to say anything because Charlotte yells, "Fine!" Her mom raises an eyebrow. Charlotte lowers her voice and says, "Okay, Mom. You win."

Her mom seems to ignore this and says why don't we go upstairs and she'll bring up the cookies when they're finished.

Charlotte gives her mom a look, which her mom also ignores, and then Charlotte grabs my arm and pulls me out of the kitchen, through the living room, and up some stairs that lead to a loft. I sit on the couch while Charlotte goes down the hall and returns with her hair pulled back. "Sorry about that," she says. But I don't know why she's apologizing because it's not that big a deal.

"It's nice your mom comes home from work and bakes cookies for you," *and is alive*, I feel like adding. My mind returns to Mom's eerie phone call.

"Oh, she doesn't work," Charlotte says as she turns on the TV. "She's here all the time." She mumbles something else, but I don't hear it. Home all the time? I can't relate. I sink into the couch and look around. Here I am with perfect Charlotte VanderKleaton in her perfect house with her perfect mom baking perfect cookies, and yet, I can't shake off my shitty mood. Why can't I be able to enjoy this?

"What's wrong?" Charlotte asks after her mother brings up a tray of warm cookies stacked high on a plate with a couple of drinks. I look at them like they're grenades because they're that dangerous. If I scarf one, I'll end up eating them all. My stomach is growling because I barfed up the pizza and the cookies smell amazing. I cross my arms across my chest so my hands can't reach for one and so I can make the growling stop and Charlotte won't hear it. But, at least that's not much of a worry since another gratuitous explosion from the action movie Charlotte put on blasts loudly from the TV.

"Nothing's wrong," I answer. I know my current mood isn't her fault, but I can't keep the irritation out of my voice. She stares at me for a minute before shrugging her shoulders and biting into another cookie. Fucking cookies.

The movie Charlotte chose is pretty horrible. It seems like the only things going on are explosions and martial arts/bar fights by a group of ninjas in business suits and . . . are those aliens? It doesn't help that Charlotte is a real talker while she watches movies. She's constantly asking questions and making comments, and if you don't answer her or comment on her comment, she just repeats herself until you do. After the first half hour, I'm ready to chew my arm off. I thought for sure she would have chosen some artsy movie from a little-known director that was really deep, not the latest action flick to go to DVD. I wonder if she picked out this movie because this is what she likes, or because she thinks this is what I like. I look over at Charlotte, her eyes glued to the TV as she asks me if I think that burly guy who just kicked some ninja's ass is somehow a CIA agent or, "Wait! Cool, I think the aliens morph and take on different forms. Right? *Right?*"

"Yeah," I say.

She goes back to watching the movie, but I give up and start looking around Charlotte's well-kept home. It makes me think of a time when I saw a house being built that only had all the beams and partial walls up. It looked like nothing more than a bunch of empty little wooden compartments. I imagined the family that would move into the house, how they would go from room to room for the rest of their lives. Sleeping here, sitting there, and eating over there. Then they would leave for a while and come back to move from little compartment to little compartment all over again. It looked too small to live a life in. It made me sad to think that's how we spend our lives—in little rooms. . . .

My thoughts get cut off when the movie finally ends. Three brawls, a car chase, and a sudden appearance of a mafia king later (who may or may not actually be an alien), Charlotte declares it a four-star flick. I agree because I don't want to spend our time discussing how much it actually sucked—no plot, no story, and I could give two shits that anybody got their head blown off because the characters sucked too.

But right now I don't care too much about her terrible taste in movies because I'm happy enough sitting here next to her and seeing her smiling back at me. Now that the movie is over, Charlotte's house is quiet, except for the comforting sound of her mom washing dishes in the kitchen. It's nice, not like the lonely quiet in my house.

Maybe one day she'll tell me she loves me. I wished she loved me. I look over at her. Am I someone worth loving?

"So, I guess I'll see you in drama," she says. We get up from the couch and head outside, where we stand awkwardly on her porch. It feels nothing like the previous night. My heart sinks. I know the night's been a bust. It's my fault and I wish I could explain everything to Charlotte. Maybe I should tell her why I'm in a funk. Maybe she'll understand. Maybe she'll lean in and kiss me and make everything else go away. But I know it's too much to lay on her. It would be wrong to taint Charlotte's perfect world with mine and everything associated with me. She'd never understand, and even if she did, who wants to be around somebody else's crap? Even now, she must think I'm some kind of depressing leech that sucks the fun out of everything. I look down at the floor, wondering if maybe I'm just reading this all wrong.

"Okay," she says, shifting her weight from one foot to the other, "so, see you Monday?"

"Yeah, right. Monday," I say, even though I want to reach out and hold her. I want to kiss her, just like last night, but everything's changed since then and I don't feel the slightest bit like the idiot dancing on the sidewalk last night, so I turn and leave, thinking I've just messed up the only good thing I had going.

• • •

On Saturday, I wake up thinking about Mom. Dad calls and I almost tell him about the call yesterday, about how I'm worried she might be dead, but then decide against it because what does he care? He left. But I really want to forget about it, so I grab a bag of old stale chips from the back of our pantry and sit down to watch some brainless reality TV.

After the chips, I eat a yogurt and five fudgesicles. They're supposed to be a low-cal once-in-a-while treat, but like there's anyone here to know. Anyway, after all of that I feel like a big fat loser. My jeans dig into my waste, and I can hardly breathe. I feel my stomach expanding like rising dough. I think about last night and how I made the pizza and soda come up, and I wonder if I can do it again. One minute it was there, and then—poof—it was gone, just flushed down the toilet like it never existed. It was so easy.

I go to the bathroom and lean over the bowl. I can do this. I stick my finger down my throat and gag a few times. I can do this. My eyes get watery. Come on, come on. I stick my finger down farther, my stomach contracting with each gag until I feel the food churning. A minute later, it makes its way out of my stomach, up my throat, and finally out of my mouth. I get that instant feeling of relief again and feel better. I go back to the couch and tuck a flannel blanket around myself supertight, vowing not to eat anything the rest of the day.

Later, I go to Ahmed's because I can't stand being in my house anymore. When I get there, Ahmed's mom answers the door.

"Hello, Cha-lie," Mrs. Bata says. Her black hair is parted down the middle and worn in a bun at the nape of her neck. "Come in," she says in her Turkish accent.

I step into their house that feels warm and smells like sweet cinnamon.

"You are just in time, Cha-lie," she says, pronouncing each word carefully and deliberately the way she always does. I like the way she says Charlie without pronouncing the *r*.

"I made baklava today. I will give you some. So delicious," she says and heads to the kitchen. "Ahmed!" she calls, "Cha-lie is here!"

I think of the junk I've already eaten today, but not

really. It doesn't really count. I follow her to the kitchen.

The kitchen smells so good and except for a couple of dishes in the sink, is in complete order. The tray of baklava sits in the center of the Batas' yellow kitchen table.

"It is still warm," Mrs. Bata says. I sit down as she grabs a knife and cuts into the crunchy, flaky, syrupy sweetness in front of us.

"Hey, what's up?" Ahmed says as he comes into the kitchen.

He looks at his mom and me, and I suddenly feel as guilty and sheepish as if Ahmed had just caught us in a long, passionate kiss. But he just looks at the baklava and grabs a piece.

"I thought you weren't supposed to eat this," he says, shoving it into his mouth.

"Oh, sorry, Cha-lie. I know you are very healthy now. That's good," she says, cutting one of the squares in half for me. Ahmed grabs another piece. My face turns red. Even though Mrs. Bata has seen me at my heaviest, I still feel embarrassed whenever my weight comes up.

"Ahmed!" she chastises as he reaches for another. "Not so much. You need to be healthy, too, like Cha-lie," she says.

"You know, baklava tastes very good with fruit," she says as she grabs a banana and starts slicing it up. She puts it on a small plate, along with the tiny half of a baklava square. She sets it in front of me and pats me on the head. If I were a cat, I think I'd be purring.

"No more for you, Ahmed," she says as she walks out of the kitchen. She speaks to him in a harsher tone than she uses for me. Secretly, I love it and secretly, I love Mrs. Bata. I feel guilty that on more than one occasion, before I ever saw or met Charlotte, she was mainly the focus of my fantasies.

"So what's up, player, you okay?" He can tell something's up. He grabs another piece of baklava. Thanks to Ahmed, I am very well versed in the difference between player and playa.

"Playa," Ahmed had explained to me one time, is the urban-street butchering of player. Player is a class A cat who knows how to take a chance, take a gamble, you know, play the game of life. A playa is a bastardization of the original definition and refers to a guy's game with the opposite sex. So while a playa might know how to play the ladies, he is by no means as sophisticated as a player. "Never say playa, Charlie. Always say player. It's not a mistake, my man, it's an educated decision." The first time he came at me with that, I was like, Holy Bat Balls, Batman! If Ahmed put that much thought into class, he would probably get As instead of Cs.

I shrug and take a small bite of the tiny piece of baklava. The sticky nuttiness melts in my mouth. I don't look up or respond, so he changes the subject, and that's why Ahmed, who eats junk food by the pound in front of me without even thinking how much it sucks for me, is my best friend.

"Hey, guess what? That extreme sports show is on," he says without waiting for me to respond with, "What?" I wonder why people say guess what when they don't really want you to guess. "I just saw a guy bust his freakin' knee. The bone was sticking out and everything! I can't believe they showed it, but they kept replaying it and then zooming in and out, in and out." Ahmed goes on about the stunt the guy was pulling and what went wrong, growing more excited by the second.

He jumps off one of the kitchen chairs and starts acting out the faulty stunt. He rolls on the floor in slow motion, holding on to his knee and fixing an exaggerated look of pain on his face. I finish the banana.

"Come on, I've got it DVR'd." He jumps up and we head to his room. After more unsuccessful attempts to get me out of my funk, he finally says, "All right, my man, lay it on me. What's the deal?"

"Forget it," I tell him as he starts bouncing a basketball off one of his walls.

"Spill it," he says. I know he means it, but I just don't feel like delving into all the ridiculous wrongness in my life.

"It's a bunch of crap, dude, forget it."

I know I should tell him about it, or them, or however you quantify all the things that suck right now, but there's too much. I don't even know where to begin nor do I want to deal with it.

Ahmed shakes his head and shrugs his shoulders. "Fine." I feel like a jerk.

I zone out and stare at the extreme sports show, which Ahmed supplements with a running commentary, and it eventually makes me crack a smile every now and then. After about two episodes, I start feeling slightly normal.

At around 9:00, I finally feel good enough to head back home. Mrs. Bata sends me armed with baklava for

Dad, which I decide to dig into right away since he's not home to enjoy it. He shouldn't get any of Mrs. Bata's baklava anyway. It's dark outside and just quiet enough to make me feel a bit jumpy and unsettled on the walk home alone, especially when I think of how I thought I saw Mom's ghost yesterday. But . . . no, I'm just psyching myself out. I walk faster anyway and unwrap the baklava, not letting myself think about how I shouldn't eat it. I take a bite and polish off the first square and then wrap up the rest for later.

My mouth and stomach yearn for more. I look at the foil in my hand. I shove more in my mouth, relishing the taste. Two minutes later, it's all gone. I crumble the foil in my hand tighter and tighter. I come home to an empty house and go to bed.

CHAPTER NINE

Charlotte acts completely normal on Monday, and I breathe a sigh of relief. Maybe Friday wasn't as bad as I thought it was. Maybe it only seemed that way because of Mom's call. Maybe I still had a chance with Charlotte.

Mrs. C is talking, but I'm not paying attention because all I can think about is how I can't screw things up with Charlotte anymore. If I were smooth, I would ask her out on a real date—like to dinner and a movie or something. But I don't have the nerve because even though I think she'd probably say yes, I can't take the chance that she might say no, especially with how I might have come off to her Friday night. Besides, a real date requires food, and right now, I don't know if I could even control my eating in front of Charlotte. I imagine her horrified face as I reach for my eighth slice of pizza, apologizing even as I stuff my mouth. No, it's better to just hang out.

So I tell her about how I haven't really started on Killinger's photography project except for some random shots and how that sucks because it's a big deal and I really like photography and blah, blah, blah, but I finally get to the point. I ask her to go scouting around and take pictures with me. And thank God, she loves the idea and tells me to meet her at her house after dinner. I head to the parking lot feeling like I'm on my way to making things okay again.

After dinner, I go to Charlotte's and she answers the door. I follow her inside.

"Come upstairs to my room, I just gotta grab my camera," she says. My palms start to sweat. I've never been in a girl's room before. Never. I have no sisters, friends who are girls, no friends with sisters, no girl cousins (or guy cousins since Mom and Dad are both only children)—hence, no girls' rooms. And now I was going to see the room of Charlotte VanderKleaton.

I imagine her room must be green. She'd never go for something typical like pink or purple. And there are probably all kinds of really cool Charlotte things in it, like a guitar. And her shelves are probably filled with really good books that no one else understands. And her walls are probably lined with posters of bands that no one has ever heard of before. And on her dresser there must be rows of strawberry lip gloss.

She opens the door.

"Sorry about the mess," she says as we trek through clothes, an overturned bowl of popcorn kernels, headbands, and shoes. "Guess I should've picked up but . . ." She looks down the hall. "It's kind of, uh, out of spite."

Her room is actually yellow—bright, sunny, yellow, with a pink and purple border.

She looks at me, sensing my disapproval, and rolls her eyes.

"My mom insisted on decorating my room, and it

wasn't worth fighting over. Anyway, this," she says, motioning to the mess, "is just to piss her off and keep her out. Not that it matters. She comes in here and goes through everything while I'm gone, then leaves it pristine, and I get a lecture on what a slob I am as soon as I get home." She studies my face. "You think I'm a bitch, don't you?"

"No, I get it," I say, though I'm struck by the irony that Charlotte has to try to keep her mom away while mine can't seem to get far enough away. . . .

"I guess if I kept it clean, it wouldn't be such an issue. But it's the principle, you know? It's *my* room. But I think she just thinks . . ." She looks up at me and shakes her head. "Forget it. It's so dumb."

I want to tell her it's not, and to keep going. But instead she plops onto her bed and I sit next to her and then I forget what I was thinking about because I realize this is where Charlotte VanderKleaton sleeps. This is where her body lays, in girl pajamas . . . or no pajamas. I quickly realize that I should stop thinking about this.

Think of dead bunnies—dead bunnies, dead bunnies, dead bunnies, and . . . Ms. Gripper's feet. Ms. Gripper has the grossest feet. It's not like I go about noticing people's feet, but hers you can't miss. I can't believe she wears sandals to school. They're all rough and crusty and one toe is missing a nail. That does the trick.

"So, what do you wanna do?" she asks.

"Thought we were gonna take pictures," I say and hold up my camera.

"Oh, right!" Charlotte gets up and rummages through her top dresser drawer. I think I saw lace panties. And it's almost too much. I mean, the only time I've ever seen underwear like that is on headless mannequins in department stores, and even then it gives me the slightest rush that makes me feel like I'm some sort of sick freak. But these are *Charlotte's* panties. That *she* wears. *Holy crap, Charlie, get a grip! Grip . . . Gripper's feet, Gripper's feet, Grippers feet!*

She pulls out a camera and shoots a picture of me before I can recover. She cracks up, so I laugh, and I just hope she's forgotten about the other night and what a drag I was. Because maybe if I got up and walked over to her right now, she'd let me kiss her.

She looks at me expectantly, and I know she's waiting for me to do something. *Get up and kiss her,* I think. But I can't because being in her room makes me nervous and I can't help wondering how much she would let me kiss her, or if she would let me do more—and exactly what that "more" would be. And I know I'm over thinking this. I should just get up off my ass and kiss her already. But I don't. I look down and fiddle with my camera instead, letting the only chance I have pass me by.

"So, let's get going then," she says. Damn it.

We head to the park and Charlotte starts snapping away. But I take a little more time trying to find something to photograph. A bare tree catches my eye. I lie down on the grass and shoot its bare arms reaching out for the sky. I review it in my digital screen. Not bad. Charlotte comes over and does the same.

"Hey, that's pretty cool," she says, reviewing her own picture.

I wonder if I could do a nature thing. But dead trees? It's nice and all, but probably at least three other students will do the same thing—the whole bare and desolate theme. I look over at Charlotte who is taking a picture of her shoe. And then I get an idea.

I could take pictures of her for my project. She seems just right in this setting, exactly what I imagine her to be: perfect. Maybe I could capture the whole oneness with earth thing. Maybe it's not the most unique idea, but I figure I can give it a try.

I tell her about my idea. At first I think she's going to love it, but for a second, I see a strange look cross her face. Did I weird her out? Does she think I have creepoid tendencies? But just as quickly, it's gone, and she starts gushing about what a great idea it is and how flattered she is to be my muse. She starts chattering away about what we should do, but I'm not really listening because all I can focus on is how great her face looks and how lucky I am that she's here with me.

• • •

The next day, Charlotte and I decide to head back to the park to take more pictures. Yesterday I'd gotten this pretty cool one with her hair flung up in the branches of this tree so the strands look like branches too, and her head is turned to the side so you see the profile of her face. And before I print it, I'll adjust the contrast so she is completely blacked out and all you can see is the bright sky and black tree with the outline of her face and her wild crazy hair strung up in the branches. Then everything together will give the appearance that the tree has a face. (I also made sure not to get too many good photos so I'd have an excuse to hang out with her again today.)

Right before we head to the park, Mark and Danny pull up in Mark's car and get out with big stupid grins on their faces. Charlotte skips over to them.

"So, Chunks, you ready?" Damn him and the whole Chunks thing. Did I miss something?

"Ready for what?"

"Tomorrow's the big day," he declares. "I'm baking tonight!"

Oh.

Danny and Mark high-five each other, and Charlotte makes a face.

"Oh my gosh, seriously?" she says. "Are you really actually doing that?"

"Yep, wanna come over for a taste test?" Mark asks.

Charlotte rolls her eyes. "Don't be a jerk."

The sting of Charlotte's words is visible on Mark's face.

"Just kidding," he mumbles, "about the taste test, not the baking. That will be funny. And you promised you'd help, Chunks, so be ready." He gives me an evil grin and plops down on Charlotte's front steps. "So, what's the plan, kids?"

He's in no hurry to leave. He knows whatever the plan was, it didn't involve him, but now he's going to make sure it does.

"We were just heading out to take more pictures for Charlie's photography project," Charlotte answers.

"So, you're into photography, Chunks?"

Yeah, shithead, I am. Do you want me to cram my camera up your ass?

"Uh, yeah, it's cool," I say.

"He's really good," Charlotte says and smiles at me.

"Aw, real sweet, Chunks. You gonna be one of those wedding photographers or something?" He glares at me and laughs before returning his attention to Charlotte. "So, Char-Char, Danny and I were just heading to the mall to hang out. Wanna come?" he says, smiling sweetly at Charlotte.

"Nah, I'm gonna work on this with Charlie. But I'll call you later."

Mark tries to hide his disappointment by shrugging his shoulders, but it's still obvious. "All right," he says. They head out and he gives his car a few revs while looking at us before peeling out of Charlotte's driveway.

Charlotte and I walk to the park, but the whole thing with Mark makes the outing feel crappy because I can't help thinking about what I'm expected to do tomorrow. Then, in the middle of shooting Charlotte, I look up at the sky and can't help remembering Mom's eerie phone call again. But I'm determined not to screw it up today, and I force myself not to think about it.

I keep taking shots of Charlotte and pretend that the way she keeps posing for the camera isn't frustrating even though it is. I don't want to capture Charlotte acting. I want pictures of how she is when she thinks no one else is watching her. I want to tell her to be herself and to stop trying so hard, but I feel funny telling her what to do, so I just keep snapping away and hope that I can get a couple of decent shots. When Charlotte pulls out a mirror to touch up her makeup, I know it's time to quit. She looks a little embarrassed when I tell her we're done. I might have hurt her feelings, but she recovers quickly, flashes me a smile, and starts talking about how much fun she had as we walk back to her house.

• • •

True to his word, Mark hands me a brownie wrapped in a plastic bag the next morning. He tells me to do it early so we can laugh at her the rest of the day. I stash it in my backpack for first period and try to think of why I should go through with this. I don't think it will even be that funny. So Tanya will walk around like a space cadet. Big deal. Everyone already thought she was a big weirdo anyway. So Mark will get the satisfaction of pulling yet another prank on her, like I care. So Charlotte will think I'm cool and fun and more like Mark. Images of the way Charlotte smiles at Mark flash through my head. Did she actually like him?

But then I think of the way she smiles at me, the way she chooses me, sometimes over Mark. Why would she do that if she didn't really like me? I feel miserable and by the time first period is over, I've talked myself into a pretty serious depression. The bell rings, and I head over to my locker. Tanya's already there. It's now or never, but I don't want to do it. I really don't. And yet . . .

"Hey," I mumble to Tanya when I get to our locker. I take out a couple of books, not caring which ones they are. I shove them in my backpack and take out the plastic bag.

"Want some?" I say, holding the bag out to her. She looks at it, and then at me, then back at the brownie.

"A brownie?" She narrows her eyes. It's the first time I haven't seen them supersized. "Why?"

She knows something's up.

"I'm just asking," I say and stand there feeling awkward as she eyes the bag suspiciously. I can almost see the cogs turning in that big cuckoo-clock head of hers. Of course she can figure it out. Of course, Tanya, someone who's been shoved down, pushed around, and humiliated on a daily basis since the third grade would question any random act of kindness and see it for what it really is.

"Well?" she says. I try not to make eye contact, but her eyes are hypnotic in the most disturbing way. And then I realize what a shitface I am. This is stupid. Why the hell did I agree to it? For Charlotte? Was this what she really wanted? Someone who could pull off some crappy prank? Sure, Tanya is pretty much a certified freak, and it's not like this could possibly damage her already infamous reputation, but she doesn't deserve this. And I don't want to do it because I'm not even sure why I'd be doing it. I don't think it would suddenly make Charlotte choose me over Mark anyway. I shove the brownie in my pocket and shake my head.

"Forget it," I tell her. She gives me a dirty look.

"It's stale," I try explaining to her. "I shouldn't have offered it to you. I . . . just, forget it."

"You're a jerk," she says and stands there like she's waiting for me to refute it, but she's right. I am a jerk. And now Tanya knows just how much of a jerk I am, a stupid, clumsy jerk at that. Even though I don't care what the spaz thinks, it still bothers me.

"I know," I say to her and shrug my shoulders. "Sorry, okay?"

The bell rings, but Tanya stands her ground and keeps staring at me. It makes me feel sheepish and uncomfortable and since I'm in no mood for a show-down, I turn to leave and ditch the brownie in the trash as I walk away. I can feel Tanya's big owl eyes blaze into my back.

After photography, Charlotte is outside Mr. Killinger's class waiting for me. My heart soars at the idea that she's there for me, but then she grabs my arm and leads me away from the classroom door abruptly.

"What did you do with that brownie?" she whispers frantically. It takes me a minute to switch gears.

"I threw it out," I tell her.

"In front of Tanya?"

I nod. Charlotte sighs loudly. "Great, well, the little nark must have fished it out somehow, and she turned you guys in. Guess who just got suspended?"

"Holy crap," I whisper. "Mark?"

"Yeah, because they checked his locker and, well, they found stuff. Anyway, I think you're next," she says, her eyes looking at everyone who passes by. "He told them you gave the brownie to Tanya."

Oh crap. . . .

"But . . . she didn't even know. She didn't eat it," I tell her.

"But she saw you throw it out!" She looks around nervously. "Listen, don't mention my name at all, okay?"

she pleads. "I'll get in trouble for just knowing about it, and my mom will have my ass! Please, don't mention my name, okay?"

She looks pretty scared. Actually, she looks terrified, just like how I feel.

"I know Mark didn't say anything about me, so . . ."

"Yeah, of course I won't," I tell her, setting her somewhat at ease but still scared shitless for myself.

"What am I gonna do?" I ask her, hoping she'll have some sort of miracle answer.

She shakes her head. "This was such a stupid idea. Now we're all gonna go down because of Tanya Bate!"

"No, not because of Tanya, because of Mark and his shitty ideas," I tell her. I'm pissed because I'm finally fed up with the fact that she doesn't see what a dumbass he is. "And I'm the one who's gonna go down."

She nods and looks down at the floor. "I'm really sorry, Charlie." I shrug my shoulders.

"Forget it," I say.

"I'll see you later, okay?" she says, "Hopefully?"

"Yeah, hopefully," I mumble. She turns away and gets swallowed up by the crowd. I take a couple of deep breaths and decide to act as normal as possible. *Just go with the flow*, I tell myself, *do what you always do*.

CHAPTER TEN

I t happens during my next class. The dean, Mr. Gouche (aka Mr. Douche), whom I've thankfully never had reason to speak to the whole three years I've been at Kennedy High, stands in the doorway and barks my name to the teacher. My body feels like I've just been jolted with a million bolts of electricity.

"Come with me," he says as he leads me to his office. When we get there, he motions for me to sit down.

"So, Grisner," he begins, managing to squeeze his enormous frame behind his tiny desk. The way he looks reminds me of a cartoon. "I heard some stuff. I'm gonna be straight with you as long as you're straight with me. I checked your file, talked to some of your teachers, and you seem like a good kid, so I know you'll be honest with me, right?"

I swallow hard and nod. He continues with his interrogation.

"You know a Tanya Bate?"

"I share a locker with her," I tell him. My voice comes out shaky. I clear my throat. He makes a note on a yellow legal pad.

"What about Mark Delancey?"

"I've hung out with him a couple of times. He's

friends with my, uh . . ." What exactly was Charlotte? My girlfriend? Friend? Girl I know? Shit. I'm not even supposed to mention her name. "With some other people I know."

He nods. "But you guys aren't friends?"

"No, not at all."

"Okay." He makes another note. "Well, here's the thing, Grisner, someone came to us and told us they heard Mark had cannabis in his possession." He studies my face. I swallow hard.

"Cannabis, sir?"

"You know, weed, pot, marijuana . . . ," he barks, like some drill sergeant. The way he's talking and the fact that I'm nervous as hell makes me want to crack up because that's the typical reaction when you're up shit's creek, right? To laugh? At least for me it is. So I bite the inside of my lip, hard.

"Right." I nod.

"However, when we questioned him," he says and then pauses for effect, "he mentioned your name in the conversation."

"Me?" I ask, with what I hope is an appropriate amount of shock. I bite my lip harder. While I know this isn't funny, I can't help but want to laugh. And I'm terrified that if I do, I'll never stop and will just be on the floor, roaring with crazy laughter from now until eternity.

He nods and waits.

"Sir, I would never . . . ," I begin. "I don't . . ." But I'm supposed to act like I don't know what I'm being accused of and I don't want to mention the pot brownie unless he brings it up. I take a deep breath and look down because I can still feel a Joker smile wanting to spring across my face.

"Well then, why would Mark single you out?" he asks.

I can't tell Mr. Gouche that this is probably a monumental occasion when in fact Mark did actually tell him the truth or that Mark hates me because for some crazy reason the girl he likes sort of likes me back or that Mark in general is an asshole and likes to make everyone's life miserable.

"I don't know. . . . I mean, he's kind of a jerk, and he doesn't like me so . . ."

He waits for me to say more. I don't. We sit in silence for a long time, and it takes every bit of my strength not to laugh as Mr. Gouche uses his superhuman dean-ray vision to look into my soul and figure out if I'm telling the truth or not. In order not to laugh, I start thinking about Tanya. There was something in the way she looked at me that stuck with me. What was it? It was kind of like . . . *you too?* Was that what it was? It makes me feel shitty. I look up at Mr. Gouche. If he knows about the brownie, he can bust me. I deserve it anyways.

Mr. Gouche takes a deep breath and sucks his teeth.

"All right, tell you what I'm gonna do," he says finally. "I'm gonna take your word for it this time," he says, "and only because you've never wasted my time before, and well, we already checked your locker because we can do things like that. But I've got my eye on you, Grisner. And I don't want to see you here again."

He scribbles a late pass.

"Now get out of here," he says and throws the get-out-of-jail-free card my way. I grab it and get the hell out of there.

I tell Charlotte everything in bits and pieces during drama. She thanks me for not mentioning her name and is glad I'm not suspended, but wonders how I managed to get out of it.

"I don't think Tanya mentioned the brownie," I tell her. "Honestly, I don't even think this whole thing went down because of her. Mr. Gouche said someone tipped him off about Mark's locker, and then I guess he called me in because Mark started blabbing about the brownie or something and he mentioned my name."

"Weird," she says.

"I know," I tell her because without a doubt the tipster was Tanya. I mean, it was the perfect revenge. She'd put the pieces together and figured it out. Afterall, it doesn't exactly take a genius to know that being offered a "homemade" brownie isn't a good thing when you're the school pariah. But I don't tell Charlotte this because she's still Mark's "friend" or whatever. And Mark is the one who mentioned my name, not Tanya. So what all this means is I pretty much owe Tanya a big one. And I don't want to give Charlotte any information that she can go back and relay to Mark, which also means I guess I don't completely trust Charlotte. Which basically . . . sucks.

• • •

That afternoon, I'm still thinking about the whole thing with Mr. Gouche and Tanya when I open our back door that leads to the kitchen and I suddenly see them—little white cartons of Chinese food stacked in the middle of the table. And there's only one explanation of how those little cartons of fast food that haven't been in our house for the past two months got here. It's Mom.

Wherever she goes, whatever she does, the way she comes back is always the same. Mom slips back into our lives after days, weeks, or months of being gone, like she just stepped in from taking a breath of fresh air. She always brings some kind of culinary peace offering—baked goods, ice cream, pizza, or cartons of Chinese food. I hear her footsteps as she comes into the kitchen.

"Hey, honey. Wow, you look great!" she says, all no-big-deal-like as she comes into the kitchen. Her hair is chopped short, and all I can do is stare. For as long as I can remember, Mom has had long, brown hair. Now it's maybe two inches from her scalp and so dark it makes her face look pale and small.

"Mom?" She comes over and gives me a hug. I pull back faster than I mean to because even though I'm relieved she's okay and not dead, I still get weirded out when Mom comes back. I don't know what to feel or how to act because I'm relieved and pissed all at the same time. And this time is especially weird because of what's going on with Dad. So I just stare at her speechless.

"What?" she asks and then her hand flies to her head. "Oh, yeah, needed a change. What do you think?" she asks. I say nothing because I can't believe she's really here in this house after two months of being gone, after the phone call just a few days ago, and after what Dad has done.

"I know, it takes awhile to get used to," she says

when I keep staring at her hair. "Anyway, are you hungry? Or . . . well, I guess maybe we should wait for Dad." She crosses her arms across her chest and bites her lip when she mentions him.

Wait for Dad? Like we're a big happy family? Like she didn't leave for two months because he's cheating on her? What the hell is going on? Did they make up and Dad didn't tell me? Was that business trip he got back from yesterday really a trip to visit Mom and plead with her to come back?

As if on cue, the front door opens and then closes.

"I'm home early for once, Sport!" Dad yells as the tapping of his shoes on the hardwood floor comes closer to the kitchen.

"Hey, Doug," Mom says as Dad appears in the kitchen doorway. He's looking through a bundle of mail in his hands.

"Carmen . . . ," he says. He stops abruptly, turning his attention to Mom, and then puts the rest of the mail on the counter. He doesn't say anything about her hair.

"How . . . are you?" Her hand flies up to her hair and smoothes it down. She walks over and gives him a hug. He looks awkward and uncomfortable, and I can't believe she's hugging him or talking to him or that she actually came back.

"Sit down, guys. I brought food."

"Of course you did," Dad says.

"I already ate," I lie.

"But sit with us," she pleads. I sigh and sit down.

My stomach growls. On the table there's lo mein, fried rice, General Tso's chicken, sweet and sour chicken, and *man, how much did she get?* It smells so good and makes me feel like some kind of animal. All I want to do is shovel it into my mouth and fill the emptiness inside the pit of my stomach.

"Come on, come on," Mom urges as she busies herself opening more cartons and getting plates.

"Charlie, aren't you going to have at least some?" she asks when I don't serve myself any food. She breaks apart her chopsticks and stares at me.

"Carmen . . . don't, please," Dad starts.

"What? Come on, it's a celebration, sort of, and besides, it's not good to deprive yourself of things," she says, looking back at me. Celebration? What the hell would we be celebrating?

Dad snorts.

Mom gives him a look. The air gets heavy and thick.

"I'll have some of the rice," I say loudly before either of them can get into it. Mom starts to scoop some of the fried rice onto a plate.

"No, white rice," I tell her, "and those vegetables over there, the ones with the least amount of sauce." She shrugs her shoulders, scooping heaping spoonfuls of food onto my plate.

Mom tries to make conversation. She's doing her usual "everything's normal" routine. Whenever Mom comes back, I can tell she feels sheepish or embarrassed or sorry even though she never says so, and she tries to cover it up by talking or laughing too much, and, of course, by bringing food home. And she always studies Dad's face trying to figure out if she's forgiven. She's doing it right now—forcing big smiles and laughing even though no one else is. She's acting the way she always does, and Dad is acting anything but remorseful. Which means she must not know. She has no idea that Dad is cheating on her. But I do, which makes everything worse than usual, because now I have to keep his secret, which he doesn't even know I'm keeping. It also means that she left us for the same reasons she always leaves. She doesn't want to be with us.

I move the food around on my plate, and Dad grunts an answer from time to time. After awhile she gives up. I guess this is our way of punishing her. Why should she ask us about things here at home? If she really wanted to know, if she really cared, she would stay. She wouldn't pick up and leave for no reason and then come back like it's no big deal. We sit in a terrible awkward silence—so silent I can hear the crunch of Dad chewing his broccoli, the scrapes of his fork and mine on our plates.

Finally, Dad finishes up and goes to his study. I hear the door close and the click of the lock. I start to follow his lead, but then halfheartedly offer to help clean up. Even though I'm upset with Mom, I also feel bad. If anyone should be feeling terrible, it's Dad. He's a big ass for letting her sit out here feeling like everything's her fault—and leaving me to deal with it. Even though I know better, I wish the food she brought would have somehow had us all talking and laughing and feeling better. But it didn't—nothing ever will. I wish I had talked more or answered her questions about fat camp and school. I wish I had said something, anything, so she wouldn't be sitting here looking like she wishes she hadn't come back. Why do we do this? Why do we make her feel unwelcome? Why couldn't she want to be here?

"Just leave it," she says when I pick up my plate. Her voice sounds flat and I feel like there's something I want to say to her—something I have to say to her—but I don't know what it is, so I just go upstairs and leave her at the table all by herself. I head to the bathroom and quietly retch up all the food I just ate. Then I go to my room and close the door and try to forget the whole night by closing my eyes and listening to music. But I can't because she's really back now. It seems like she's been gone for years, and everything's changed since she left. I don't know how we all fit together anymore. Things are far more screwed up than ever before. I know stuff I wish I didn't know, stuff she doesn't, stuff she can't know. And I can't decide what's worse. Mom knowing or Mom not knowing. I pluck the earplugs out of my ears because I can't stand the music anymore, and I put a pillow over my head because I can't stand the quiet in our house.

CHAPTER ELEVEN

I try to act normal and go about everything the way I always do, but it's not the same. School drags on. Ahmed gets on my nerves. And instead of being happy when I see Charlotte, I'm depressed, even when we go scout out more places to take pictures. Nothing is the same when Mom is home. I don't feel like myself at school or at home. It's like having a stranger visiting and staying at your house. When I walk into a room and she's there, I don't know what to say to her and I'm constantly thinking of a reason to be somewhere else. Dad has gone completely AWOL. He leaves before I wake up and comes home long after I've gone to bed. I understand why he does it, but I wish he would stick around. If not for her, at least for me.

One day I get home just as Dad calls and he says he'll be late. Mom sounds pathetic on the phone, telling him she made his favorite, then sounds annoyed when she can't get a specific time of when he will be home. I don't tell her I had planned on skipping dinner when she serves me a heaping bowl of spaghetti and meatballs she made. She serves herself some, too and we sit down.

For once, she's not talkative. She eats quietly, not looking over toward me. I look down at my plate and chew slowly, willing myself to eat only half. I imagine taking the pot full of marinara and meatballs and hiding out in my closet while I gorge on it all by myself. Lately I've been hungrier than usual and the diet crap I'd fooled myself into believing could fill me up, doesn't cut it. This is what I want. I want to scarf it down and stuff more in until I'm full, so full that I can't think or move or speak. I abandon my plan to eat only half and end up stuffing a whole meatball in my mouth. It'll be easy enough to get rid of later.

"More late nights," Mom mutters suddenly and shakes her head as her voice trails off.

The way she says it makes my stomach turn. Could she possibly know? If she did she would die—or maybe she would kill. Would Mom be one of those people who kills their spouses in the heat of the moment? Would she get off by reason of insanity? She couldn't find out. I couldn't let her find out.

"Mom." I choose my words carefully. "Dad really missed you this time," I say.

She looks over at me. Does she believe me?

"I mean, he always does, but this time he kept talking about all these things he wanted to do together once you got back."

She bites her bottom lip and stares out our kitchen window. "I . . . ," she starts, but she doesn't continue.

"He told me he wanted us to go camping at Morrow Mountain State Park like we did that one time, remember?"

She nods her head and pushes the plate of food away from her. She looks confused and fragile. I remember thinking Mom used to be, like Mr. Killinger said about his mother, a "free spirit." The way she seemed to blow in the direction of the wind. The way her mind hopped from this to that. Now I don't think Mom is a free spirit. The thought makes me sad. I take another bite of food.

She brushes her hair with her hand and looks over at me. "Really, Charlie?" she asks. She's looking at me, and I can barely meet her gaze. I swallow hard and do the worst thing I've ever done.

"Yeah, it's all he's talked about," I say. "I'm surprised he hasn't mentioned it to you yet. Maybe because he's been working so much. You know, he took some time off to spend with me while you were gone."

She takes a deep breath and smiles. She sits, then nods her head, and kind of laughs. The creases on her forehead disappear, and suddenly, she looks soft and vibrant and the happiest I've seen her in a long time. I can't believe the transformation from that one little lie. I should be happy that I can offer her this one moment of peace. But it's the shittiest thing I think I've ever done, and I hope I go straight to hell for it because that's what I deserve. I shove a forkful of spaghetti in my mouth.

She gets up from the table and comes around behind me. "I don't know what gets into me sometimes," she whispers and kisses the top of my head. "I should know better. I'm wrong about so many things so often." She pats my shoulders and walks over to the sink to wash dishes.

Maybe I didn't even hear right the other night. Maybe there was no forbidden conversation coming from

Dad's den. Maybe there was no whispered "I love you." The hushed words float to my ears. No—there was.

I look over at her and then quickly look away because staring at her back, watching her wash the dishes and listening to her hum happily to herself makes me feel terrible and like at any moment I'm going to yell, *You're right! It's true! You're not crazy . . . about this!*

I shove more food in my mouth. I can barely eat it, but I do because if I don't, those words will come up, and I'll end up telling Mom the truth.

Later that night, Mom goes out of her way to do nice things for Dad, and I feel sick to my stomach each time. I've just made a fool out of her. And it continues the rest of the week. She bakes his favorite stuff, buys him new shirts and ties, and talks about taking a camping trip to Morrow Mountain. But he's indifferent and distant, and I can tell Mom doesn't know what the hell to make of it. It's my fault. It's my fault that Mom stares at Dad the way she does, so hopeful. And then her face turns from hopeful to hurt when Dad announces one night that he has business in Chicago and has to fly out the following day. I can hardly handle the way she looks when he leaves

• • •

Charlotte and I hang out during drama as usual, but something seems off. I try to make small talk, try to listen when she talks, and try to laugh when she jokes around with me, but it doesn't feel like it used to. This is the girl who is supposed to save me. This girl is supposed to make everything better, but she's not. Maybe she's already given up on me and that's why things seem different. Maybe she's made her final choice between me and Mark.

I walk around feeling terrible about Mom and Dad and Charlotte until one day, on our way home from school, Ahmed finally says, "All right, cat, I get it. I know your mom's back and I told myself I'd give you a week, but your week is up and you need to stop feeling sorry for yourself and get back in the game."

"I'm not feeling sorry for myself. And you have no clue, okay? So drop it."

Something in my voice makes Ahmed look at me sideways as he navigates the Roller Skate to my house. "Okay, sorry. But . . . you know what I mean."

I don't snap at him again, so he goes on. "You gotta step up and be a player, get it? You gotta live, Chuckie. You gotta go be a pimp. You gotta do something that'll counter your funk. Like go up to Charlotte and say, *chickie, I claim you, you dig?* You can't sit around like this and let everyone suck the life outta you."

Ahmed is my best friend, my only friend, but I really feel like shoving his own car up his ass. It's easy for him to say this since he doesn't know all the shit I'm going through. But even though he doesn't know everything, some of what he's saying makes sense.

"Maybe you're right, but I just gotta get things straightened out, you know? I'll be fine, dude. I just need . . ." I shrug my shoulders because I don't know what I need. I look up at my house and dread going in.

"I gotta get some work done on Killinger's project. Wanna go with me to the botanical gardens?" I ask since I need some nature shots. I also really need to get started on superimposing Charlotte's pictures on the other ones to get the effect I want. And maybe it would help get my mind off of things.

"Charlie, that's fruity. Listen to Ahmed," he says. "You're gonna go in your house, and you're gonna give your baby a ring-a-ding. You two are gonna hang. You're gonna smooch, and you're gonna feel better. Trust me. Besides, I have a date," he says and grins.

"What! Who the hell with?"

"This new girl who showed up in my ceramics class. Daisy. Isn't that a fantastic name? I always wanted to date a chickie with a name like Daisy. Anyway, she's no Janie Hass, but she's cute and digs my style. I started talking about Frankie and the boys and she told me she idolizes Sammy." He's acting very, very smooth, but suddenly he can't contain himself. "And I'm psyched, brother! I mean a girl who idolizes Sammy!" He hits the steering wheel a couple of times. "Out of this world, know what I mean? Can you believe it?"

"No, I can't, and why didn't you say anything?"

"I just did, man, anyways, it's not a big deal. Just another chickie." He smoothes out the wrinkles in his shirt and adjusts his cuffs.

"Right, well, good luck," I say.

"Thanks. See you tomorrow," he yells as the Roller Skate zips away. I feel a little jealous as I watch him go, which doesn't make sense because I have Charlotte, sort of.

I'm still wondering why the hell I feel jealous as I head inside my house. I pass the door to Dad's office, and it's opened just enough for me to see inside. My heart starts thumping quickly as I scan the rest of the house from where I stand, but nothing else seems out of place. I go into Dad's office, even though part of me is telling me to get the hell out of there since somebody's obviously broken in, but I already know there's only one person who could do this. Mom.

Every drawer of Dad's desk is opened; all the papers that are ordinarily tucked away in folders and stacked on his desk lie all over the floor, along with picture frames, pens, pencils, tacks, paper clips, and rubber bands. A framed picture of a duck that for whatever reason, was one of Dad's favorites, is broken on the floor with a three-hole punch near it that was apparently the weapon. But the worst thing, what actually scares me most, is the couch. Dad's brown leather sofa is slashed. Long gashes reveal the yellow, foamy stuffing inside. It looks like a skinned animal that vultures tore up.

I suddenly hear the frantic *bump, bump, bump* of footsteps upstairs. "Mom?" I call out as I head up the stairs. "Mom!" I yell again. Her bedroom door is closed. I try to open it, but it's locked, so I bang on it.

"Mom, are you okay?" She doesn't respond, but I can hear her inside. "Can I come in? Mom, please let me in." But there's no answer. The craziness of the couch makes me wonder what else Mom can do—would do.

The footsteps continue from her room and then to the bathroom and back to her room and back to the bathroom. I wonder what she could be doing.

"Mom, come out, please. I . . . we can go get dinner," I say because I don't know what else to say. "You know what would be good?" I rack my brain for things to continue to say. I need to keep talking so that we don't get swallowed up in silence with only those frantic thumps for sound. "Pizza. We could even make it if you want. I saw this cooking show and it's not that hard." I wait for an answer, but there's none. Maybe I should try to pick the lock, except I don't know how. I keep talking.

"We could put a bunch of toppings on it." I can smell bleach and wonder what the hell she's doing.

"Come on, Mom. Let's go get everything. Open the door, please!" I start banging on it harder and finally it swings open.

"Charlie! I don't give a shit about pizza right now!" she yells.

She's wearing an oversized black sweater that is now stained with splotches and streaks of orangey white where bleach has splashed on it.

"I don't give two or three or four shits about pizza! Order a pizza, if you want, and fuck off!" she yells and turns back around to the piles of clothes in her room. Her words shoot out and pierce me.

I've never seen her like this and it scares me. I don't know what to do. She's never talked to me like that before, even in the worst of times, and especially not after she's been gone for over two months.

She grabs a pile of what I notice to be just Dad's clothes and walks to the bathroom. I step into the room and almost get knocked out by the smell of bleach. She comes back out for another pile, this one with some of

Dad's shoes, books, and belts, and walks back to the bathroom again. I follow, still unsure how I should act or what I should say. I peer into their bathroom and see the growing mass of Dad's belongings piled up in the bathtub. On the bathroom floor are two bottles of bleach, one opened and toppled over having already been used.

Mom grabs the other one and starts pouring more bleach onto the new additions in the tub.

"Oh my God," I whisper, even though I don't mean to say it out loud. She either doesn't or pretends not to hear me.

"Mom, stop, please . . . stop," I tell her.

"Stop? Stop? You know who should stop, Charlie? Your father, Charlie! Your father should stop! He should stop screwing some tramp in Chicago! Did you know that's why he left? On sudden 'business'?" she spits out through clenched teeth as she empties out the second bottle.

Holy shit. She knows. She stares at me like she expects me to answer, and I now know what could happen if she found out. I meet her eyes for a moment, but I can't look at what I see behind there, so I look at the heaping mound of Dad's clothes in the tub. She goes back to frantically pouring bleach on Dad's belongings, splattering more on herself, and I'm glad she doesn't demand an answer because whether I lied or told her the truth, both outcomes would have been terrible.

"Didn't know that about your precious father, did you?" she says. Even though she's standing right here, right in front of me, talking to me, it's like she's not really there. She's looking at me, but I don't think she really sees me. She's in this room, but I don't know if she knows that. Something inside of her, her brain or consciousness or whatever makes you realize right from wrong, good from bad, sane from insane just . . . snapped. And I'm the only one here to really see it.

"Well, now you know! And I know!" She throws the bleach bottle across the room, and it hits the wall and bounces off before skidding across the floor. "We all know about Kate! All these months I suspected it, and he just acts like I'm crazy! Like I'm out of my mind. But I knew, and it was killing me, so I came home and I find . . ." She starts crying hysterically. "And you, you want me to make pizza!" she says, throwing the accusation at me like she just found out I was stealing money from her. She shakes her head in disbelief.

"So this is what it comes to! Damn it! Damn it! Damn it!" She kicks the tub repeatedly, hard enough to break her toes through the flimsy shoes she has on, but it doesn't seem to bother her. She starts screaming, really screaming, which scares me even more, and all I can think is that I have to calm her down, but I don't know how, she is already beyond reach. All I can do is watch this terrifying episode.

"I gotta go," she says suddenly.

"What?"

"I gotta go. I gotta go, out. I gotta get out!"

"Mom, don't. I mean, wait. Wait until you calm down, okay?"

"No, no." She shakes her head and walks out of the bathroom and into the bedroom. I follow her. "*Now*, I gotta go now." She looks around like she's trying to figure out what to take but then shakes her head again and starts racing down the stairs. I run after her.

"Mom, please don't! Please!" I'm frantic now, wondering if I can find her keys before she can. But she's already in the kitchen, and I hear the jingle as she swipes them from the counter.

"I'll go with you! Mom, please! I'll drive, Mom! Mom!" I yell. She's already out the back door. I run after her toward the garage. The car beeps as she unlocks it. She gets in and slams the door shut, and just as I reach the passenger side door handle, I hear the lock click.

I pound on the window. "Mom, please. Don't do this! Mom, let me in!" She starts up the car and doesn't even look out for me as she throws it into drive. I jump back as she screeches away and watch her car race down the street and out of sight.

I stand there for a long time and start pacing, trying to think of what I should do. Should I call the cops? What could they do? I'd go after her, but I can't. I don't have a car. And even if I did, I imagine the craziness of me in a high-speed chase after my mother. I don't know what to do. There's nothing I can do. There's no one here to help me.

I go back inside the house, but there's nowhere to go. Nothing seems right. I pace the kitchen wondering what I should do. The TV is on in the family room. I hear a commercial for the local car dealership, and I just want to pound the obnoxious spokesperson. His voice is annoying, and I hate him. I hate everything.

I go back to Dad's office. It's like a car crash; I don't want to look, but I can't help it. I sit down on the side of the couch with the least amount of gashes and take in everything Mom has done. I notice she didn't trash Dad's computer and it's opened. I walk over and see an e-mail to Kate from Dad.

Kate,
I miss you. I can't tell you how different my life seems with you in it. I feel like I have a reason to wake up. . . .

I close Dad's laptop and pick it up. It's heavy in my hands. I set it down and open it again. I start typing.

Kate,
Thought you'd like to know my crazy mother has just gone off on a suicidal road trip. Thanks for being the last nail in her coffin. Say hi to Dad for me.
Charlie Grisner.

My finger hovers over the send button. Just a quick click and somebody would know how I really feel. I imagine some faceless woman opening this e-mail today—maybe even with Dad sitting next to her. I close my eyes and take a deep breath. I wish I could send it. I wish I had the nerve. I wish I weren't such a wuss.

DELETE

I close the laptop and send it flying across the room. I sit down on the floor, surrounded by the mess.

I can't even begin to imagine where Mom went or how to follow her, or what else she'll do. I can't believe she found out. Why isn't Dad here to deal with it? How could he do this to me, leaving me alone to pick up the pieces? I can't believe this is really happening. I contemplate calling Dad, but he can't do anything from Chicago. I don't know what to do. I have absolutely no clue. So I stare at Dad's ripped-up couch and wait.

I don't know what I'm waiting for, but I wait. And the only thing that makes me certain about what just happened is seeing the disaster in this room.

CHAPTER TWELVE

An hour later, our home phone rings, interrupting the running images in my mind of the past week—the way she acted, the way she looked while Dad and I either ignored or lied to her. I trip over all the crap on the floor as I run to answer it.

"Doug Grisner, please," says the voice on the other line.

"He's not here." He's never here anymore.

"Who am I speaking with?"

"Who is this?" I ask.

"My name is Lee from Hunter County Hospital. I'm calling because . . . who am I speaking with?"

"This is Charlie Grisner." My heart starts pounding harder. Hospital? What happened to Mom? "What's going on?" I ask as I start to feel adrenaline rushing through my legs and arms.

"How old are you, Charlie?" the guy asks. The sense that something is very wrong makes me cooperate.

"Eighteen, is it my mom? Is she there?"

"Yes, she's here."

"What's wrong? Is something wrong? Is she okay?" They wouldn't tell me she's dead over the phone, would they? Horrible images of mangled cars flash through my head—sirens, flashing lights, my mother . . .

"She's in our ER. She was brought here after officers received several calls reporting a confused and disoriented woman driving erratically. . . ."

"Is she okay? Was she in an accident?" I can barely make out the words as I remember the way Mom left here a few hours ago.

"She's all right, but there was an accident. Can you come down here now? I think she really needs someone here that she knows . . . as soon as possible."

"Yeah, I'll be there in a minute, I mean, as soon as, yeah, I'm on my way," I tell him, my mind already racing with the realization that I have no car and will have to call Ahmed for a ride. I place my finger on the hang-up button, wait for the dial tone, and dial Ahmed's number. One ring . . . two rings . . . three . . . four . . . five rings . . . and then his voice mail answers. I hang up and run to my room for my phone to text him:

Call now. Need help. Now.

While I wait for Ahmed to call, I think of someone else to call. *Okay, think, Charlie, think.* I could call Ahmed's mom, but . . . who else? I know Ahmed's mom would help me, but I didn't want to make mom seem even worse than I suspected Ahmed's mom already thought she was. It was stupid. I should just call Mrs. Bata. Mom was in the hospital, doing and acting like God knows what, but . . . was there anyone else? Charlotte? The idea leaves my mind as soon as I think of it. I already know exactly how Charlotte would look at my mom . . . her eyes wide, staring in shock at the crazy woman in front of her. No, I definitely can't call Charlotte. And then, I remember Mr. Killinger.

I sit on my bed wondering if I should call him. No, he's my teacher and teachers just say stuff like that. But if he didn't mean it, he wouldn't have actually given me his phone number. *Make a decision.* I go to my dresser and open the top drawer where I keep miscellaneous crap that I might need someday. I search for Killinger's card and find it. I take a deep breath. This is insane. But I dial his number anyway, and before I can think about it anymore, I hit the call button.

"Hello?"

"Um, hi, Mr. Killinger? This is Charlie, Charlie Grisner." There's a slight pause on the other end before he answers.

"Hi, Charlie. What's up?"

"I know this is kind of weird, but I was hoping . . . I, uh, kind of need help," I say, trying to speak over the lump in my throat that feels like it's cutting off my voice and breath.

"Okay . . . what's going on?" he asks.

"I need a ride to the hospital."

"Are you hurt?"

"No . . ."

"Charlie?"

The lump is getting bigger. My eyes burn and any minute now I know I'm going to start the kind of crying that shuts you down—makes it impossible to talk.

"Um . . . it's my mom . . ." My voice is shaking. "She's there, and I . . . they just called, and I . . . need a ride because my dad's out of town and I can't . . . ," I explain, trying to get out all the words.

"Okay . . . Charlie? Listen, just relax, okay? Where do you live?" I give him my address.

"I'm on my way," he says, and I nod even though he can't see me. I hang up and the tears I've been trying to hold back win out. It's all my fault. I knew she was too upset to drive, but I didn't stop her. I close my eyes and press my hands on them hard, crushing my eyeballs, but the tears keep coming anyway, and soon my nose is stuffed and I can't breath. My mom could've killed herself, and I would have blamed myself forever for not stopping her. I press down harder on my eyes, but I can't stop. I can't stand being such a wimp and crying like this. If I could, I would punch myself in the gut right now.

Get up and stop being a freakin' wuss! I tell myself. *Mr. Killinger will be here any minute.* I run to the bathroom to blow my nose and splash water on my face before running downstairs. Five minutes later, I see a blue Volvo coming down the road slowly. I go outside and stand by the curb. Mr. Killinger speeds up and pulls up in front of me.

"Hey, you all right?" he asks as I get in. I nod. "Is she at Hunter County?" I nod again.

I stare out the window as we drive to the hospital. Mr. Killinger doesn't say anything else, and I'm grateful because I don't think I can talk. I watch the bare trees rushing past us, the blur of dead grass, and lean my head on the cold window. I'm glad the day is gray and cold.

Once we're at the hospital, Mr. Killinger asks me my mother's name and inquires about her. A nurse leads us to a small room, where I find my mother sitting on a cot, hunched over, mumbling something to herself. The nurse whispers, "I'll be back in a minute," and she leaves us standing in the doorway. Mr. Killinger steps over to the side to give us some privacy.

I look at her, scared to go toward her, scared she might explode again. This mumbling woman sitting here, hunched over like she's scared of the world, like she's taking cover from danger, can't really be my mother. I feel the tears start to burn my eyes. No . . . this crazy woman, who makes my life hell, who makes me have to call teachers I barely know, who embarrasses me, is my mother.

"Mom?" Her head snaps up like she's just been shocked with electricity. She has some small cuts on her face and a piece of gauze on her forehead.

"Charlie?" she relaxes. "Hey, bud . . . what are you doing here?" She says it so casually, like we're at home, like she isn't sitting in the hospital after having driven into a parked car.

"Are you okay?"

She looks confused. "Okay? Yeah, of course . . . oh," she says as her hand flies up to the bandage on her head, "this. It's nothing. I'm fine." She looks at me and smiles. If I wasn't so mad at her, that smile would have broken me because she looks so sad.

"Mom," I say, but my voice doesn't work. What was she thinking? Why did she do this? And why did she always make me feel so guilty? Even when she's the one always screwing things up, I'm the one who always feels bad.

An old man with glasses and a white coat comes in. "Hello," he says and smiles. Why was everyone so cheery? Why was everyone acting like nothing had happened?

"I'm Dr. Yan and you must be Charlie," he says. I look at him. "I just spoke to your friend out there," he explains. "Well, Charlie . . . your mom's okay. Some bumps and a small cut. She'll be just fine." He smiles at Mom. "Won't you dear?" Mom nods.

"She's not badly hurt," he says, looking in my direction, "but she was hysterical, so we gave her a little something for her nerves." Hysterical. Automatically, I look around and search for any evidence of the same thing Mom had done to Dad's office.

"So, here are some directions on how to clean those cuts and stitches, as well as some literature on . . . mental health and helpful resources." He turns and hands me all the papers in his hands. "Is your dad home?" he asks.

"On a business trip," I say. Mom starts crying, and I pray to God that the mention of my dad won't set her off again.

He nods. "Just give him those brochures there. I'll be calling him myself a little later on today to explain everything, including insurance and payment information, so you don't have to worry about that, Charlie. Does he have a cell phone number?"

I give him Dad's number.

"Okay then, I'd say you guys are all set to go. Any questions?" He looks back and forth between Mom and me. I shake my head. She smiles at him.

"Well, it was a pleasure, my dear, though I don't hope to see you here again." He laughs and takes her by the arm. "Let me help you up."

Mom looks at him gratefully. "Thank you, Dr. Yan, for everything. You know, you are very kind." Mom says this like she has to think very hard to remember each word.

"Thank you, dear. Now you just get some rest and listen to your family," he says as he leads her out of the room and into the hallway where Mr. Killinger is still waiting.

"Who are you?" she asks as she looks at Mr. Killinger.

"This is Mr. Killinger," I tell her, "my photography teacher. He gave me a ride here, Mom."

"I hadn't even thought of how you got here," she says to me, looking up and shaking her head as if to clear it. Dr. Yan hands Mom over to Mr. Killinger, like a delicate artifact, giving him instructions to hold on to her as she walks because she might be a little dizzy from the medication.

"Nice to meet you, Mrs. Grisner," Mr. Killinger says calmly as he takes hold of her arm.

"You are all so kind and helpful," she says.

I get a sick feeling in my stomach at those words. Mom clings on to Mr. Killinger as if she's afraid of sinking into the floor. I follow behind them and notice how the nurses look up and stare at Mom as she makes her way down the hall.

My phone rings as we get to the parking lot. I look down and see Ahmed's number, but I can't talk now. A second later, it pings with a new text message.

R u ok? What the hell is going on?

I don't have it in me to begin to answer that. I slide the phone back into my pocket.

Mr. Killinger helps mom into the front passenger side of his car and I get into the backseat. I watch as Mom talks to Mr. Killinger about how she hates this gloomy weather, and how she really actually prefers a warmer climate where the sun is always shining.

Another text from Ahmed:

Dude?????

I take a deep breath and type out a response that I hope will stop any more questions.

Everything's fine. Just c u tomorrow.

•••

When we get home, Mr. Killinger tries to help Mom out of the car, but I don't want him to come inside. I tell him we'll be fine, but he looks uneasy. I keep thanking him, but he still makes no move to get back in the car. Finally after I promise him that yes, I will call him again if I need to, he gets back in his car and drives away.

Mom and I go inside and she retreats to her room, which still reeks of bleach. An hour later Dad calls, but I ignore it. Why is he calling? Like he cares. Like *I* should care that he remembers us and actually picked up the phone. After several tries to my cell number, he tries our home phone, then cell again, and finally just leaves a voice mail. I listen to it, even though I wish I didn't want to.

Hey, Sport, it's Dad. I just got a call from the hospital. I'm so sorry, Charlie, I can't believe this . . . God . . . I really want to talk to you. But, okay, I'm at the airport now, and I'm taking the next flight out. I'll be home around midnight, okay? Charlie . . . I'm sorry. Really. I love you, Sport.

I resist throwing my phone across the room. Dad can shove his apologies up his ass. This house is a freakin' mad house, and all I want is to get the hell out of here—just go somewhere far away where I don't have to pick up the pieces of my mom or make excuses for my dad. Anywhere other than this suffocating, life-sucking box we live in. But it's hopeless. There's nowhere for me to go. I know there's Ahmed's house, and if he and his mom knew about all the shit that just went down, they'd kill me for not heading straight over there. But the truth is, it's hard to *constantly* have to admit how screwed up my family is. It's hard to constantly need to be saved. I don't want to have to need anyone, and I want to be on my own; I don't care where I go, where I end up, or how I get there. I just know I have to leave *here.*

And that's when it hits me. Why not? Apparently it's okay for everyone else to leave. Apparently it's okay to abandon everyone and worry only about yourself. So why shouldn't I leave? There was really no reason to stay. This isn't my mess. I'm not the one who royally screwed up all of our lives. So let them deal with it. And me, I'll take off, just like they do. I'll even leave a note; I'll let them know so they won't send out some search party or anything. Actually, screw the note. They probably won't even notice it.

I run upstairs and grab my old knapsack out of my closet. I throw in a couple of pairs of jeans, T-shirts, underwear, and socks. I run to the bathroom and grab my toothbrush. My heart is racing. Can I do this? Everything in my body tells me no, but I have to get out of here. I come across an old pack of Turkish cigarettes Ahmed swiped from his dad last year. I'd forgotten I still had them. We had tried to smoke them, but both of us agreed they pretty much sucked and made us sick. It was kind of a blow to Ahmed who thought he'd look much more Rat Packish if he smoked. I throw them in my backpack, along with my iPod, phone, and a book. I lift my mattress and grab the envelope of money I've saved up from birthdays and holidays and shove it in my pocket. I zip up my backpack and throw it on my back. The heaviness of it feels good. I keep moving so I don't have time to change my mind.

I pass Mom's door and stop. She's crying and all I can do is think of her on the other side, shut up in her room. No. I wasn't going to get reeled into this again. I couldn't think about her. I wanted to open the door and tell her to shut the hell up, but the sound of her crying makes me want to stay and help her somehow, even as it simultaneously makes me want to get as far away from her as possible. My backpack feels a hundred pounds heavier. No. They had to fix this. I'm done.

I race down the stairs and out the front door. I take several deep breaths. The cold night air fills my lungs and dissipates the heaviness in my chest. I close the door behind me, take out my iPod, crank up the music, and don't look back.

I walk out of our neighborhood and down the main road that eventually leads to another main road riddled with restaurants, gas stations, fast food places, and other businesses near Rennington College. I take out the cigarettes and the lighter hidden inside the pack. I don't know why I ever bothered to hide them when neither of my parents were ever around to find them. I could hide a prostitute in my room for a month, and they'd probably never notice. I light one of the cigarettes, inhale deeply, and start coughing. They taste like crap, but I keep smoking, and when I'm almost done, I light the next one with the end of this one and keep walking, music blaring in my ears.

I can't believe this is my life. I can't believe these are my parents. I should just live by myself. I mean, I am eighteen. All I have to do is get a job. Mom wouldn't really care since she'd barely be around to realize I'm gone, and Dad could start a new life somewhere else with Kate.

A car pulls up next to me and comes to a severe stop a couple of feet ahead. For a minute I think I'm going to get abducted, but then I recognize the car. It's the rumbling black Mustang that Mark has had since sophomore year. The passenger's side door opens and out steps Charlotte VanderKleaton. I pluck the earplugs out of my ears.

"Charlie? What are you doing?" she asks, staring at the cigarette in my hand.

"Nothing," I say. Wow, what a brilliant response.

The driver's side opens, and Mark looks at me over the roof. "I told Char-Char it was you! She didn't believe me, but I knew it was." He grins and taps the top of his car.

"Hi." I cough. I didn't exhale as smoothly as I intended.

"Charlie! Do you know how bad these things are for you? What are you doing?" She comes over and pulls the cigarette out of my hand and throws it on the ground. "You smoke?"

"No," I say as she stomps it out with her foot. Brilliant response #2.

She looks at me funny. Not like she's a prude, just . . . surprised and like she expects some kind of explanation, but I have none to offer. And although I think I'm in love with Charlotte, I wish she would just leave. Right now, she's only a reminder of all that's wrong with me. I don't want her to figure it out right here, right now—especially not in front of Mark. I stare at the ground, refusing to meet her gaze.

"Charlie?" she says. I don't answer. I can't answer. It's like my body and mind go into some kind of protective mode when confronted like this—like an animal playing dead. I can't speak. "Charlie?" she says again.

"Come on Char-Char! He's just being a baby 'cause you caught him."

"I am not!" I yell, shooting a dirty look at the prick. He laughs, satisfied that I took the bait. I look at the ground again. I can feel the weight of Charlotte's stare.

"Why do you hide everything from me?" she asks

quietly.

But I don't say anything. I just shrug and keep looking at the sidewalk.

She sighs. "Do you want a ride? We were just heading back from getting something to eat."

I shake my head. "No. Just go with Mark."

"Char, let's go! I'm gonna get a ticket or something."

"You sure?" she asks again, ignoring Mark's obnoxious yells.

I nod, but she doesn't leave.

"Charlie, what's wrong with you?" she asks. "If something's wrong, why won't you tell me?"

"Nothing's wrong, just go," I say, even though I know as soon as she does, I'll be crushed. She waits, but I have nothing else to say, so she sighs and turns to go.

"God, I just, I don't get you," she says as she looks over her shoulder at me, maybe to see if I respond. I don't and a minute later, I hear the slam of two car doors, and then the rumbling as Mark revs the gas and his car screeches away, and with it any hopes I ever had of getting Charlotte. I take out another cigarette and smoke it.

I keep taking hits from it, even as it makes me dizzy and want to puke. I'd rather feel sick than heartbroken. But it doesn't work, I just feel like an ass. My head hurts. I light up again and walk blindly to wherever.

About fifteen minutes later, I feel really sick. I break out in a cold sweat and start shaking. I feel like an idiot for smoking this many cigarettes. All the nicotine in my mouth has mixed with saliva and dripped down to my stomach making me feel like crap. I stop at a gas station and buy a bag of Doritos, a couple of cans of soda, a Snickers bar, and a bag of gummy bears. The old woman behind the counter is missing a tooth and smells like cigarettes and body odor. I try not to gag as she rings up the items. Then the terrible thought of me on the streets panhandling for Ho Hos flashes through my mind. I grab the bag and my change and get out of there.

I shove gummy bears in my mouth as I keep walking, trying to get away from the lights and businesses on the main road. When I'm done with them, I open the bag of Doritos and crunch away on those, hoping the taste of them kills the ashtray taste in my mouth. After another fifteen minutes, I've finished those too. I pop open one of the sodas and guzzle it down. I feel disgusting, and all I can think of are the horrible tastes in my mouth and the bloating in my stomach. I look around. I've never really been down this way and start getting creeped out as I go. The lights of the main road are barely visible now, and everything looks older and crappier as I continue walking.

I contemplate whether I should go back home. This is stupid. Where was I going anyway? Charlotte was right. Something was wrong with me. Very, very wrong if I was running around doing shit like this. But I don't care. So what if I was using this as an excuse to crumble and check out. If anyone deserves to check out, it's me.

I stop and find some bushes where I can upchuck all the crap I just ate. I double over and press on my stomach, making it all come up, which is easy since I already feel nauseous. I wish I had water to rinse out my mouth. I open another soda and swish with that instead, then feel slightly better. I take a deep breath and try to stop thinking about my parents and Charlotte.

It's really dark now. Only one in every couple of streetlights actually works, casting small sporadic orbs of orange below. I hear voices ahead—a couple of guys joking around. I stop, and wonder if I should go to the other side of the street. But then realize how stupid and paranoid I'm being. It's just some deadbeats hanging out on the street. I keep my head down and keep going.

"So I says to her, 'if you know so much, then you write the fucking paper, lady,' and I whipped the book so fast back at her, it hit her freaking tit." A roar of laughter and couple of high fives follow. "It was so funny man! Her jaw dropped and she was like . . . hey, hey, you!" I know the guy is talking to me now, but try to convince myself he's still telling the story as I keep walking, pretending I didn't hear a thing.

"Hey, you! Little man," he calls.

"That ain't no little man," someone else says, followed by laughing. I resist the urge to run, but speed up.

"I said, hey, you!" I hear footsteps coming up fast behind me. "You better slow down and check in, man!" I swallow hard and stop. The guy steps up in front of me, way too close for comfort.

"Eh, leave him alone, man. He's a chump." I hear a voice coming from the pack behind me.

"Nah, nah, let him tell us who he is. So?" He looks at me, but I can hardly see his face because he's standing right outside of the streetlight. I feel like I'm being interrogated. The guy is short, and maybe I could take him alone, but he's not alone. I've never even been in a fight before. Something tells me he has.

"Charlie," I tell him. My voice sounds hoarse and shaky.

"You ain't from around here. Whatcha doing around these parts, Charlie? You brought us anything?" He gives a slight nod to the other guys and suddenly I hear more footsteps coming up behind me, and I know I'm in trouble. One of them takes my backpack right off my back and starts digging through it.

"No, I mean . . . sure, take it. I'm just, I'm just going for a walk," I explain.

"A walk? You fucking kiddin' me? Hey, guys, this kid is just going for a walk." He laughs, turns back to me, and steps closer into the light. He's either my age or younger, but he looks older somehow. "Where you think you're at, huh? Fucking Sunnyville?" The other guys laugh too.

I shake my head, suddenly very aware of what a stupid idea this was coming here.

"Listen, Charlie," he says, "I don't usually do favors, but I'm gonna do you one. You don't want to hang around here. And if you wanna walk, you probably should walk right back that way, to your little suburban neighborhood, and not come around here no more 'cause the truth is, we're really not as nice as we seem."

"Okay," I say, "you're probably right. I mean . . ." The rest of the guys circle around me. My heart is pounding in my ears, and my whole body feels weak and twitchy.

"Listen, I'm sorry, I didn't mean to bother you guys." Everything in my body is telling me to run, but I force myself not to take off because if I do, these guys will definitely hunt me down. The pack moves in closer.

"Yeah, I know, but still, everything's got a price, you know?" he says.

The guy who took off my backpack says, "Payday," as he fishes out my iPod and the envelope with money.

"Anything else on you?" the first guy says. I'm still fighting the urge not to run, and my heart is pounding so hard it's getting hard to think. It's difficult to breath and the nausea from the cigarettes returns.

"I ain't got all night, man, and if you don't hand over your cash, my boys are gonna check your pockets for you, and I know you don't want that, right?" I nod and then quickly shake my head no. I dig into my pocket and take out the change the toothless woman gave me.

"Good, well . . . I wouldn't stay around here too long." He starts walking back to the car where they were all hanging out and his friends follow. "Thanks, for stopping by," he calls back and waves my money in the air.

I cross the street and start walking back the way I came from. I hurry past their stares. As soon as I'm past their driveway, I take off. I run like a little wuss. I run like I'm running for my life, which I'm pretty sure I am. I run without stopping, without seeing, without caring how stupid I must look to these guys, even as I hear them laughing and hollering behind me. I run even as my face freezes with the dumb tears that I can't control. I run even as my lungs want to explode inside my chest. I run and run and run, like a squealing pig, all the way home.

CHAPTER THIRTEEN

Dad's flight ends up being delayed, and he doesn't get home until after I get back, which is right before the sun comes up the following morning. So, in fact, my attempt at running away does go unnoticed. When he gets home, he comes into my room and sits on my bed. He just sits there on the edge with his elbows on his knees and his hands over his eyes. I pretend I'm sleeping. He whispers my name a couple of times, pats my leg, but I don't respond. I'm not about to make this easy for him.

I stay in bed most of the day, at least until Ahmed finally calls the house and asks if I want to go see a movie.

"What the hell, man, I've been calling and texting you all day," he says when I finally answer.

"I lost my phone."

"That blows."

"Yeah, long story," I say.

"So, what the hell happened?"

"Tell you later."

"You sure?" he insists.

"Yeah, positive," I tell him, refusing to go into everything right this second.

"Fine, your call," he concedes. "Anyway, you know that new flick about those old New York gangsters from the twenties? It's out now. You in?"

I don't really feel up to it, but I don't want to be confined here with Mom and Dad. I'm pretty sure if I don't leave, they are going to suck the life right out of me.

"Sure, I guess."

"Cool! One's playing in thirty minutes, so we gotta jet, like now, though. Pick you up in five minutes."

I get ready, pulling on some dirty jeans and one of my old T-shirts that is stretched out and too big on me. I look homeless, but I don't care. I'm just pulling on my sneakers when Dad comes in.

"Sport, we need to talk."

I continue tying my Converse. Talk? He can talk to my ass.

"Sport, please," he says. *Sport, what a joke.*

I go to grab my wallet and house key but then remember I got fucking mugged last night while Dad was with his girlfriend and Mom was crying in her room. I walk around, pretending like I'm searching for something. I grab a hoodie and walk out of my bedroom.

"Charlie, come back here, please hear me out."

I make a bolt for it downstairs.

"Charlie, don't walk out that door." I pull my hoodie on. Was he serious? Did he just seriously tell me to not walk out the door? The anger that has been simmering inside me bubbles up. I whip around as he comes down the stairs.

"You are the last person who should tell me not to walk out. You're the one who walked out, Dad. You and

Mom, so just leave me the hell alone, all right? Don't tell *me* not to walk out! Why don't *you* stay here and take care of her bullshit for once!" I yell before slamming the door so hard I think I may have broken it.

Even as I run down the walkway, headed toward Ahmed's, I can't believe I just said what I said. I'd never talked to Dad like that in my life. Even though it felt good to actually speak up for once, it also means I'll have more shit to deal with when I get back. At the corner I see the Roller Skate coming, then Ahmed pulls up to me on the curb.

"What's up, I thought I was picking you up?" Ahmed says as I get in.

"Yeah, I know. I had to get out of there."

"Gotcha." Ahmed speeds away. He starts to talk about the premise of the movie.

"Hey, how was your date?" I cut in, trying to sound normal.

"Cat, I didn't even tell you! Girl is a poser. She didn't know any Sammy flicks, which is fine, you know, I don't discriminate. But she kept acting like she knew who he was. So I made up some fake movie and said he was in it, and she was all like, 'oh yeah, I loved that one!' I mean, be real, you know? I think she wants to hang out more, but it's not in the cards."

"Sorry, man, that sucks."

He shrugs his shoulders. "It happens. What about you? Did you hang with Charlotte?"

When he mentions her name, I think of last night and how I ran into her on the street. How I undoubtedly screwed up the already slim chance I might have had with her—and to make things worse—I looked like an asshole. The same feeling I had from smoking too many cigarettes last night comes back. But she was always hanging out with Mark anyway. If she actually liked me, what the hell was she doing with him all the time? None of it made any sense, and I needed to talk about all this like I needed a hole in the head, but I ask Ahmed anyway.

"So, be honest, okay?" I say.

"Always am, my man. What's up?"

"You think Charlotte's a poser?"

He rubs his chin and considers this a moment, which makes my stomach sink.

"That chickie's hard to figure out," he says finally. "Honestly, man, and I know this might hurt, but you said be honest." He looks over at me. I nod.

"Basically, I think she's genuine enough, but I also think she digs both you and Mark, and she's just gonna keep hanging with both of you until one of you gets tired of it and calls her out on it."

"You think I should call her out on it?"

"I don't know." He turns real serious for a minute. "I mean, if you feel about her the way I felt about, you know, that one who did me wrong and shall remain nameless, then I get it."

"This sucks," I say.

"I know it, cat, I know." I don't say anymore since this conversation is pointless. I don't think Charlotte and I will be hanging out much more. We ride in silence for a little while. Then I remember I can't pay for my movie ticket.

"Dude . . . you're gonna have to spot me. Some modern-day gangstas mugged me last night."

"What?" Ahmed looks like he just got hit with a taser.

I sigh and just start explaining. At first I wasn't going to say anything, but I figure I might as well. I'm too tired to come up with anything but the truth. So I tell him about Dad's affair, how Mom went crazy, and how I had to pick her up at the hospital with Killinger. And then I tell him how I headed into no-man's-land and got a pretty little mugging after running into Charlotte and Mark. Ahmed just keeps looking at me like I'm out of my mind. The really strange part is that even after I explain all this craziness, it doesn't even seem *that* strange or wild to me anymore, which is probably crazy in and of itself, but whatever.

"Holy shit, Charlie . . . I mean, HO-LY SHIT! Are you seriously carrying all this crap around with you? And you're asking me about my freakin' date? Why are you just telling me this now?" he yells. I shrug.

He looks at me with his eyes as big as Tanya Bate's, which almost makes me laugh. "You should've come to my house," he says.

"In my defense, I didn't know I was heading into a fucking rumble with Ponyboy and company, and yes, I should've, but I wasn't thinking straight after the whole thing with my mom."

"Yeah, I know," he says and nods like he gets it. "But still, you better freakin' unload immediately from now on. I'm serious. We're best friends, Charlie. Solid, you dig?" He looks over at me.

"Got it," I say, and for a moment I contemplate

whether I should tell him about throwing up, too. But I can't. When I think about me bent over the toilet, with my face in the crapper like that, it makes me feel pathetic. I don't think I can say it out loud.

We get to the theater, park the Roller Skate, and get our tickets before heading to the concession stand where Ahmed buys a large tub of popcorn, and I hint that maybe he should get a couple of the king-sized chocolate bars too. He does, as well as the drinks I suggest we'll need to wash it all down with. My mouth starts watering as we carry the food to our seats. As the theater darkens for the previews, I open the pack of Reese's Peanut Butter Cups and shove one in my mouth.

The movie starts. I cram popcorn in my mouth and slurp away on my soda. I'm glad Ahmed is too engrossed in the movie to notice how much I'm eating. The movie is pretty good, and even though there's a lot of shooting and gore, it's not bad—not like the crappy movie I saw with Charlotte. A feeling of dread washes over me when I think of her again. I eat more junk until all I can focus on is how the food is making me feel stuffed. I can't stand the feeling of it sitting in my stomach. Then I'm consumed with the thought of all the calories I just ate. I don't want to care, but I do. I know I have to get rid of it. I can't pay attention to the movie anymore until I do.

Halfway through, I get up and go to the bathroom. It's empty. I lock the stall, retch it all up fast, and start to feel better.

•   •   •

I stay at Ahmed's house that night, the next night, and through the weekend. Dad calls a bunch of times, and even though Mrs. Bata pleads with me to talk to him, she tells him I won't come to the phone. I overhear her counseling him to give me some time—that she'll take care of me. I seriously consider asking her if I can move in, but actually, seeing the perfectness in Ahmed's house starts to depress me. So I finally decide to go back home. Even though I don't want to deal with Dad yet, part of me just wants to get it over with already.

I start making the walk back home. I turn my corner and from here I can see the garage door is open.

The rental car, which I know Mom got while her car was in the shop, is gone now, but her car isn't there yet. And I know it means she's gone, again. I stand still on the sidewalk for a while and stare at the empty garage.

I don't think I can do this anymore. I still can't decide if I should thank God that she's gone and I don't have to deal with her craziness, or if I should want her back, despite having to deal with her craziness. I don't want to go any closer to that mess. I look at the sky, and wonder if there really is a heaven. I don't think there is, but if there is, I wish I could go there now. Or maybe the earth could open up and swallow me, and I could become part of this concrete sidewalk. Maybe I would turn into a weed that sprouts up between the cracks. I wish I were a weed.

I look back in the direction of Ahmed's house. But I've already been over there too much. I wonder if I should go see Charlotte, but I shoot down the idea as soon as it enters my head. *Just go home*, I tell myself.

The truth is, no matter where I go for a distraction, I'll still have to go home eventually. I take a deep breath and head toward the insane asylum.

When I open the door, Dad immediately comes to the foyer.

"Okay," he starts before I have a chance to say anything, "so I know you're pissed and you have every right to be. But we gotta talk."

"I already know she's gone again," I say.

He sighs and drops his head. "I'm sorry, Sport. Can we sit down?" he asks looking at me still standing in the front doorway. I close the door but don't move.

"Please."

It's not that I'm being spiteful, really. I mean, sure I want to make this hard for him. But I don't move because I can't. I actually would rather sit, sink, and disappear into the couch, but my feet don't move—just in case I need to make a run for it again.

"Fine." Dad sits on one of the bottom steps and rests his arms on his knees. "I know things are messed up, Sport. And, yes, Mom's gone, and I don't know where she went. Again." Are we really talking about this? He looks up at me and waits for me to say something. My throat is closing up.

Maybe if you weren't cheating on her, she would stay.

"Charlie," he starts again, "I made a huge mistake. I . . ." He can't bring himself to actually say it, and I can't bring myself to let him off the hook. I wait silently.

"I knew from the start what I was doing was wrong, there's no excuse for it. And it did contribute to Mom leaving, this time. But Charlie, she's left so many times before, you know that. She just goes. It's always been that way, ever since I met her." I know it's true, but I wonder if it was always *this* bad. I try to remember exactly how often she left when I was younger, but I can't. Was she really always this way? How much worse had it gotten? How did he—we—miss it?

I look at Dad who looks like he's wondering the same thing. He sighs. "I don't know, maybe I thought I could save her somehow. Maybe I thought it would change, if I loved her enough." His voice cracks. "Sometimes, it didn't seem so bad, but . . . ," his voice trails off. He waits for me to say something, but I don't.

"Sport . . . ," he starts. And it's so stupid, but that's what sets me off. That's what makes me not able to listen to him anymore. Hearing him call me Sport over and over again.

"Just leave me alone, all right? And stop it with the Sport crap, okay? Why do you call me Sport, anyway? I hate it! I hate that nobody ever calls me Charlie!" I head up the stairs, past him, and up to my room. He looks crushed as hell, but I don't care. I just want to stay mad.

I try to sleep, but I can't. I lie down in my dark room and stare at the ceiling, trying to make sense of everything. I don't know what to feel. I don't know what's right or wrong.

I start wondering if maybe I'm an orphan and imagine that my real parents are out there in the world somewhere, still miserable because they lost me. Maybe we were on some camping trip when I was really young, and I woke up early one morning and went wandering in the woods by myself. And maybe I stumbled upon Doug and Carmen and they told me I was miles from the campgrounds and they would take me back. But they didn't because they simply could not part with me. And since Carmen bribed me with chocolate frosted doughnuts, I never asked about my real parents again. Maybe my real dad invented . . . I don't know . . . the Internet because he took all his pain and desperation and channeled it into tracking down his long lost son. And maybe my real mom . . . God, what would she be like? I can't picture her. I don't know why, but I can't. All I see is Mom. . . .

CHAPTER FOURTEEN

The day before Thanksgiving break, Mr. Killinger reminds us that we should already be working on the final touches of our collection. This sucks. I only had those shots of Charlotte that I hadn't done anything with because they hadn't turned out how I thought they would. And now I didn't have the nerve to ask her to go scouting anymore because even though both of us pretend like the other night on the street never happened, I know things aren't totally right with us.

"Hey, Charlie," Mr. Killinger calls over to me after class as everyone files out of the room. I stay behind. "How are you? How are things at home?" he asks casually as he puts stuff away around the room.

"Cool." My standard answer.

"Really?" he asks, raising an eyebrow.

"Yeah. Mom's gonna get some help, and I'm pretty sure she's taking some kind of medication. I think she'll be okay," I lie. Even if I wanted to, how the hell could I even begin to tell him the truth? "She's already cooking for Thanksgiving, making a bunch of pies." I roll my eyes and half smile, surprised at the lies escaping my mouth, lies I wish were true. "Even bread pudding. Bread pudding is my favorite." *Shut up, shut up, shut up.* "She feels bad after everything, so she's making all our favorites. She's usually not like that, you know?" *SHUT UP!*

Mr. Killinger presses his lips together and twists his mouth the way people do when they don't really believe what you're telling them. It looks like he's pondering whether he should press me more on the subject.

"Yeah, I understand." He studies me. I meet his look, putting on my most honest face. "Well, I'm glad things are getting better," he says. "So, have you talked more with the counselor here at school?" As soon as I saw Killinger at school after the whole incident with Mom, he told me he'd had to refer me. I had talked to the counselor guy but just told him some lies that I guess he didn't bother to look into, and I pretended everything was getting better.

I nod. "Yeah, I did and it's really helping. Everything's fine. Thanks," I tell him.

"Well, I'm here, too, you know. You can talk to me whenever." I nod. "So, how's your project going?"

Damn. I used up all my creativity for the Thanksgiving lies.

"Have you finished it yet?"

"Sort of, but . . ."

"Having trouble?"

I shrug and decide to be honest about this because it's easier than coming up with more crap. "I really don't know what it is. Taking pictures usually isn't difficult for me. What I was working on didn't really turn out the way I wanted it to."

The pictures I'd taken of Charlotte sucked. I had

uploaded them, but they didn't look right. When I look at Charlotte, in those rare moments she's not talking a million miles an hour, in the time when she's done saying something and just stares at me before looking away, I see something different. And I was sure I could capture that in the photos, or at the very least, in just one of them. But I hadn't. And I don't know if it's because I imagined it, or if I suck, or because now the pictures of her are hard to look at, but they weren't working.

"Well," Mr. Killinger says while leaning on his desk and crossing his arms, "the idea doesn't have to be earth shattering, you know. It's the execution of it," he says and tells me how every picture says or conveys something. "It's not about conventional beauty," he says. "It's about the meaning or message behind the picture, and that might be pretty or ugly or disturbing or raw, but it's that honesty that makes a picture . . . memorable, striking and even shocking. Pictures should make you think, Charlie, reflect, ponder, in the same way that a good song or book or painting does." Mr. Killinger sometimes gets too passionate talking about photography, but I listen to him, even as he goes on and on because there's something in his riddles and rambling that makes sense. It makes me think, and by the time I'm headed to lunch to meet Ahmed, all I can think of is the project because Killinger's words have triggered some images and ideas. But none of them are of Charlotte.

• • •

Later that night, I'm home staring at the outline Mr. Killinger handed out the first day of class, which states all the requirements for the project. Killinger's words keep ringing in my ears. What do I have to say? And I think of how it always seems like I have a lot to say but can never form the words to get it out. But it's there, always, whatever I have to say, it's always in me, stuck in the back of my throat. Sometimes I think I'm choking on it. Whatever the shapeless words are, whatever inexplicable things I have to say, they're killing me.

When I go to sleep, Killinger's words are still floating around in my head. They say sometimes your brain works things out subconsciously, without you even being aware of it. And maybe that's why, as I'm falling asleep, I suddenly see it all so clearly. I see my whole collection. At first I'm startled, and it knocks the freakin' wind out of me, it really does, because it's amazing and bad and good and crazy and real and everything I've ever felt but never had the words for. But I don't know if I can do it. Could I actually make those pictures real for everyone to see, for everyone to talk about or criticize, or worse, laugh at?

I feel like one of those freaks on trashy talk shows, keeping some kind of terrible secret from someone, but then go on national TV and tell them in front of everyone so all these strangers can be entertained by their pain. Is that what I was thinking of doing? But I can't think about those TV people right now because I have to do this. I jump out of bed and start writing down my ideas before they float out of my head.

I wake up early, even though I'm not sure if I actually fell asleep last night, and get to work immediately. I work on what I can before I have to ask Dad what I really don't feel like asking him. But I figure he owes me, which is probably the only way I'm going to get him to do what I need him to do.

"Hey," I mutter as I enter the living room, where he's sitting with a bag of chips watching a football game. He looks up and quickly puts away the chips.

"Hey," he says. We stare at each other a long time before I finally blurt out, "I need you to do something for me."

"Anything, Sport." He shakes his head. "I'm sorry, I mean Charlie." He offers me a weak smile. I nod. He's trying.

"But . . ." There was no way to make this not sound creepy. "I, uh, you can't ask me why, just know it's for a really important school project. And I, um, I really need you to just agree, okay?"

"No questions?" he asks.

"It's just easier if you don't ask."

He looks apprehensive. I look down at my sneakers and wait for an answer. "Okay, whatever you need."

"Thanks," I mumble, "uh, just wait here. I'll be right back."

"Wait, now?"

"Dad."

"Right, no questions."

I nod and head upstairs for one of Dad's button-down shirts, a black handkerchief I can use as a blindfold, and the red lipstick I got from Mom's bathroom. My heart is beating like it's gonna quit any minute, and until I actually start doing this, I'm not sure I can go through with it. I open the lipstick, sure that this will damage my psyche more than everything with Mom, but put it on anyways before I can change my mind, and then kiss the collar of Dad's shirt. I quickly wipe off the lipstick, but no matter how hard I scrub, my mouth still looks slightly red. Great.

I head downstairs and choose a spot for the photo shoot. I scan the living room, bring in a white sheet to use as a backdrop, move here, move there, change this, change that, mumble to myself, until finally I'm satisfied. Dad looks bewildered and stares at my mouth. But I don't care. I have to get this done before I change my mind. I ask him to put on the blindfold, and only after that, ask him to put on the shirt. And true to his word, he doesn't ask questions. I snap a bunch of pictures and even as I snap them, I know they're turning out perfect. I try not to look at Dad directly, just from behind the lens. From here, he's not my dad. From here, he's just some guy, who looks scared and lonely and guilty and tired. From here, he's a guy I kind of start to feel bad for.

"Okay, we're done," I say. He takes the blindfold off and then the shirt. He notices the lipstick on it, but doesn't say anything. "Now, one more thing," I say. He nods. "I need some money so I can get a tripod. I have to take a couple shots of myself." He reaches into his pocket and pulls out his wallet. He looks defeated.

"And when I get back I . . . I need to work down here . . . by myself. You can't walk in, so . . ." I almost feel bad the way I'm calling the shots right now, but then I don't.

"I got it. I'll hit the road for a while." He puts his wallet back in his pocket. Then he asks, "Are you okay?"

"Yeah, don't worry. I'm gonna call Ahmed and get a ride to the store."

"I could take you," he offers.

"No, it's okay. I'll call Ahmed. And . . . thanks. I'll see you later," I tell him as I race upstairs.

Ahmed carts me around, and I feel guilty not asking him to stick around while I work on the project, but it's better if I do it alone. I'm anxious to get it done and see how this crazy idea turns out. After Ahmed drops me off at home, I head toward the kitchen with the chocolate doughnuts and three-pack of white crewneck T-shirts I've just purchased. I try not to pay too much attention to the fruit logo on the packaging and get back to work by smearing chocolate frosting on the front of one of the shirts.

When I set up the tripod and put the blindfold on, it feels weird. I grab the doughnut resting on my lap and shove it halfway in my mouth. I feel small and unreal, like I'm all alone in a dark box. One that anyone could open at anytime while I sit in the center of it, fully exposed. The back of my head and neck are tingling. Even though I've never really been scared of the dark, I want to tear it off as soon as I put the blindfold on, but I force myself to sit there, counting the clicks of the camera until it's over. I wonder if they will come out right. I wonder if I look like Dad. I wonder if what I'm doing makes any sense.

Finally, there are a few sharp clicks and then no

more. I spit the doughnut out and reach to take off the blindfold, but I decide to sit there for another minute, maybe an eternity, making myself feel the panic, the loneliness, the dark, even though I feel like I might explode. And the longer I sit like that, the more I begin to wonder, is this how Mom feels? I sit there a little longer until I can't take it anymore and finally rip the blindfold off. Everything is too bright. I take some deep breaths and will myself to relax until everything looks real again.

• • •

On Thanksgiving, Dad is depressed. I can't blame him; I'm feeling pretty down too. All I can do is think about Mom and us because my photos force me to look at how we all really are. The picture I took of Dad flashes through my mind. Normally I can tell he never wants to see what he doesn't know how to fix. But in the picture, when there's nothing but darkness, it's like he's forced to face what he doesn't want to see and can't ignore it. On the other hand, when I think of the pictures I've taken of Mom in the past, it's different. It's like she's completely absent—or worse, maybe she's empty. And I don't know how to fill that emptiness. I don't think Dad knows how to either, which makes this all really scary.

At first, I wonder if Dad and I are just going to pretend it's not Thanksgiving, especially after Mrs. Bata calls and invites us over to her house and Dad kindly declines. But at the last minute, Dad mumbles that he'll be right back and leaves. He then comes home with a ready-made rotisserie chicken, instant mashed potatoes and stuffing, frozen corn, and a pumpkin pie—which is Mom's favorite. He heats everything up in the microwave and sets it all out on the table. By the time the potatoes are done, the stuffing is cold, and the corn is shriveled up. It's sad, especially with the untouched pumpkin pie in the center of the table like that. I sit, barely eating anything, and for the first time in forever, I realize, I'm not dying to stuff my face. All I can think about are the pictures and all the work I still have to do. My stomach isn't throbbing with the usual pain only food can fill. I'm not starving. And I wonder why.

After Dad realizes that Thanksgiving pretty much sucks, after we've moved our food around on our plates long enough, and after we've stared at the untouched pumpkin pie, I disappear back upstairs to set up the last picture. The rest of the break that's all I do until I have all the pictures I need. The seven pictures that tell our story.

CHAPTER FIFTEEN

Ahmed picks me up on Monday and I can tell he's a little irritated that I blew him off the rest of break after he chauffeured me around to get supplies.

"I had to get my project done, man," I tell him, a little irritated myself. After I uploaded all the images, and cropped, blurred, and adjusted the black and white, they finally looked exactly how I wanted, I think. I kept flipping through them and started thinking about the whole TV talk show thing. The pictures were not pretty, not happy, not your typical family portraits. Instead, they're pretty scary, making me feel sick and excited all at the same time. Like I just did something amazing . . . or horrible . . . or amazing. I kept going back and forth all night, thinking and rethinking, getting out of bed and looking at them again. Whenever I started to get used to the images, all of a sudden I saw them with fresh eyes, and I couldn't believe I was going to turn this in.

"I'm so gonna sound like a chickie right now, but just, you know," Ahmed says as he shrugs his shoulders, looks over at me, and continues, "are you okay?" he asks. I realize he's not so much irritated as he is actually worried, especially after I unloaded on him the other week and stayed at his house; I haven't really checked in with him since.

"Yeah, I'm fine," I tell him. "Really."

"All right, but you got a place to crash if you need it," he says. "Seriously, anytime and for as long as you want. I mean it." I know he does. "And now to counter that previously total chickie statement, I gotta say, you look like shit, man," he says.

"I know."

"I'm gonna have to lend you some threads. Do a makeover or something."

"Makeover? Oh, okay that's not a chickie thing to say or anything." We start laughing, and then can't stop the rest of the way to school.

When I get to Killinger's class, I realize I'm nervous again. It's one thing to see those pictures on my computer knowing I'm the only one who has seen them, but the thought of someone else looking at them scares the crap out of me. As we shuffle in, and everyone disperses to the computers to upload images or print them, or to their desks to start framing or working on their artist's statement, I head to my seat and sit down, concentrating on taking deep breaths.

"Still having trouble?" Mr. Killinger asks as he comes up next to me.

"I, uh, I have, it's . . ." I can't get the words out so I just take out my flash drive and hold it up to him. He looks at it.

"You got them? All of them?"

I nod.

"Wow, that fast? Well, want me to take a look?"

My heart races faster. This is not normal. People don't get this freaked about stuff do they? I really feel like my whole body is going to shut down.

"Charlie? Do you want me to take a look?"

No . . . yes—I don't know.

I nod.

He takes the flash drive from my hand, heads to his desk, and sits at his computer. At least nobody else will see it. I don't move. I just watch his face as he searches for the file, and then, I can tell he's found it. His mouth opens slightly as he looks through the pictures . . . for a long time. The noise in the room starts sounding far away. My ears feel like they're suddenly on fire. I can't tell if the expression on Mr. Killinger's face is good, bad, shock, awe, or confusion. I feel like a little kid about to get in trouble. Maybe it's not okay for me to do what I did. Maybe you're not supposed to out your family like this.

Finally he looks up and over to me. He nods, which I think means *okay, what you did is okay*.

At first I'm very reluctant for anyone to see them, but it's impossible for everyone not to since we frame all of our pictures in class. I get the same reaction each time: someone looks over my shoulder and there's a long pause, before they finally say something. Mr. Killinger says that's good. It shocks in a raw, honest, thought-provoking way, but it seems like it shocks them more in a *this kid is a freak* kind of way. Eventually though, it gets easier, especially when they tell me it's really good. And I think they mean it. Then I start to actually believe them. I look at the kids in my photography class, all so very different from one another: Punks, Preps, Loners, Stoners, Ordinaries . . . and yet, we're sort of the same somehow. This hiding behind the lens and snapping things maybe others don't see, we all have it in common. It's important to us.

As the week goes on, as everyone shows me their collections, like mine, their photos somehow tell me things about them I'd never known. I feel a strange sense of belonging. Part of me doesn't really care about winning, but then after I set up my exhibit in the school's theater for judging, I start to wonder—and hope—that I do have a chance.

That Friday during class, Mr. Killinger drops the bomb on us.

"So," he starts as soon as the bell rings, "just want to let you know that there's a new procedure for choosing the winner."

Everyone stares at him.

"You won't actually know who has won until the night of the exhibit."

"Aw, man, Mr. Killinger. That's total cheese. How's the winner supposed to set up his collection at Rennington if he doesn't know he's won?" Steve-O Carter yells from the back. He thinks everything is cheese, but he brings up a good point.

"Hang on. Actually, it's pretty cool. As you all know, preliminary judging started yesterday here at school, which is why all of you set up your collections in the theater. Well, the judges were so floored by your talents, they decided to showcase the top three collections at Rennington instead of just the winner as originally planned. There will still only be one scholarship, but at least two more of you will have your work displayed at Rennington."

Steve-O perks up and listens. So does the rest of the class.

"And the scholarship recipient will be announced on the night of the final exhibit."

The room is buzzing. Cheese or not, everyone was excited and wanted to be one of the three finalists.

"When will we know who the three finalists are?" someone asks.

"Right now," Killinger says, and he whips out a note card from his back pocket. People start to hoot and holler. Mr. Killinger waits for silence. Everyone begins to hush each other.

"In no particular order," Killinger begins, eyeing us and pausing for dramatic effect, "Lisa Wakefield." Lisa squeals and everyone claps. Mr. Killinger waits.

"Steve Carter," he booms again. Steve-O jumps up on a table and pumps his fist in the air. Everyone cracks up and then starts shutting each other up. Mr. Killinger waits again.

"And finally," he says. Everyone is waiting, people are whispering please, please, please.

"Charlie Grisner," Mr. Killinger booms. Someone slaps me on the back and congratulates me. I take a deep breath, unsure of how to react. Because even though I'm happy, and this is awesome and everyone is congratulating me, I've had enough experience to know the laws of the universe for Charlie Grisner. I know things like this don't happen to guys like me. And when they do, it always means something bad is going to follow.

• • •

I don't get a chance to tell Dad about being a finalist because he's not home when I get home, but Ahmed, of course, tells his mom who insists we celebrate, so she prepares a meal of brown rice with amazing spicy chicken, vegetables, and yogurt sauce (that she prepared very healthy, she tells me quietly).

After dinner, we all watch some Turkish movies that Ahmed and I laugh at and his mother and father shush us without really meaning it. And Ahmed starts imitating some Turkish dance that he integrates with pop lock moves, and Mr. Bata gets up and starts imitating him, and Mrs. Bata laughs until tears come out of her eyes. It's the best time I've had in a long time, and I laugh so hard my stomach hurts. I feel so much a part of a family that it almost doesn't matter that it's not my own. It's just great to laugh, to feel a part of something, a part of others. I can't remember if I'd ever felt that with my parents. I don't think I have, which suddenly makes me sad, but I keep laughing with the Batas, join Ahmed and his dad, even though I can't shut out the thought of my parents. I go home wishing I were Turkish.

CHAPTER SIXTEEN

The following Monday I head toward my locker when I start noticing people staring at me. I wonder if word got out about me being one of the finalists in the photography competition, but nobody else really cares about that, so it seems unlikely. I keep walking and become acutely aware of whispers and giggles around me. I feel like Moses as people make an open path for me as I get closer to my locker. I know this can't be good. And then, I see them.

There weren't many, but enough that anyone who walked past my locker would see them. So here it was, Mark's revenge for the pot-brownie failure that led to his suspension, and for Charlotte showing interest in me. I picture Mark's smug face and his words from the other day ring in my ears. *So, you're into photography, Chunks?* Motherfucker.

The picture was obviously from an ad cut out of a magazine. A black and white of the beach, water foaming as it spills up onto shore on two bodies pressed and entangled in each other, they looked more like one body with excess limbs. The lovers look as if they just washed up on shore, exhausted but miraculously unscathed and unharmed from some boating accident, and are reveling in the refuge of each other's arms after a perilous adventure.

Except the girl's face is not that of a supermodel. It's Tanya's zitty face superimposed on the model. And Tanya is clinging on to and laying on top of me. My face—no— my face from last year had been carefully cropped and perfectly positioned onto the body of the male model. And as if that wasn't enough, there are captions.

"Oh, Chunks, thank you for saving me. Oh, Chunks, your body is so muscular. Oh, Chunks, Oh, Chunks . . ."

"Hush, my precious, and kiss me. I will protect you forever."

The craftsmanship was incredible, the idea typical, and yet the blow . . . catastrophic.

I stare at the pictures. They decorate my locker like wallpaper. My face looks like a big, puffy, pale pastry— glistening like it's been glazed—my eyes are two small raisins, and the smile the photographer had forced me to do makes me look like I'm taking a dump. It was by far the worst class picture I'd ever taken . . . and now, Charlotte would see it. I wish I could die.

There I was. That was me. That ugly, doughy, loser boy was me. Who was I kidding? It didn't matter if I lost the weight, if I strutted around like I was someone new, or if I was a finalist in some stupid photo contest. That right there, staring back at me with the most miserable face in human existence, was the real Charlie. That is who I'd always been, who I'd always be—miserable, scared, ugly, fat Charlie. The bell rings. The ringing laughter and whispers around me eventually fade, but I just stare. I can't move.

I hear the squeak of sneakers behind me and Tanya appears out of nowhere. Great, just the person I want to see. My face gets hot with embarrassment.

"Watch out," she says, sighing loudly.

I move, hoping she'll just grab her books and leave. She rips all the pictures off and crumbles them up in one big heap. She walks over to the trash can and tosses them in like it's no big deal. And I guess for Tanya, it's not. This is just another typical day in her crappy life. Does she even realize her life sucks?

"Just forget it," she says. "Mark's a real dumbass, and all his little admirers are a bunch of mindless minions. Don't let it get to you." She looks at me. I spy what might be sympathy and understanding in her big owl eyes. "I guess this wouldn't be the best time for me to tell you that the turd-head taped one of these on the back of every bathroom stall in the school." She pushes up her glasses in true nerd fashion before opening the locker and trading out some books.

My stomach drops. She says it so matter of fact it makes me want to smack her. And suddenly I'm pissed.

"What is wrong with you?" I ask her.

"What?"

"What is wrong with you?" I repeat, louder this time. "I mean, I guess it's because you're already a freak, right? You just don't care, right? Because you're better than all these people?"

She cocks her head to one side and stares at me as if trying to analyze me. It only pisses me off more.

"But I don't want to be a freak," I tell her. "I don't want to be 'better' than all of these people." My words spill out before I can plug them up. "I want to be like them. And I would be if I weren't sharing a locker with you. But . . . it's not like anything could go my way just once, right? And your powers are so great, Tanya, so astonishingly great that I've been tapped a freak by association!" I yell at her, knowing that what I'm saying is not true, that I was a freak long before I shared a locker with Tanya, but I don't care because it feels good, it feels good to yell at someone, to blame somebody else for my fucked-up life.

"My God, I actually felt sorry for you," I yell. "But I don't know why. You do nothing to try and fit in. You love that people look at you weird, that they ostracize you. Look at you," I demand. "Look at you!" I shout until she actually looks down at her grubby sneakers and stretch pants.

"You know what? You're an idiot!" she spits out. "You want to be one of these people? Why? Because they're so fantastic? Because they can cut and kill people like you and me if we let them? Wake up, Charlie."

"I am NOT like you!" I yell back.

"YES, you are! You may hate it, and you may fight it, and you may think it's the worst thing in the world, but I'm telling you, you are EXACTLY like me and someday when you're far enough from the disease that is this shallow, kill or be killed school controlled by a bunch of zombies, you're gonna realize that, and you know what? You're gonna be glad you're like me!" Her face is red and blotchy, and I just want to punch her and make her shut up. Instead, I hate myself even more for being such a wimp.

"I hate you," I say.

"You hate yourself," she spits back, "and that's worse. Get over it, Charlie, or you're seriously gonna be fucked up." She stares at me with her big owl eyes like she feels sorry for me. She feels sorry for *me?*

And that's the last straw. I've sunk so low that Tanya Bate feels sorry for me.

I get the hell out of there—walk right past the lady guard at the front of the school who supposedly makes sure no one escapes this prison. Instead she's sleeping in her golf cart. I walk home and ditch the rest of the day. It doesn't matter. Nobody's home.

I mope around until Ahmed stops by after school and tries to convince me it's not that big a deal.

"Come over. Mom said she'd make another great dinner. We can watch Turkish movies and free-style again." He jumps up and does one of the Turkish pop lock moves he invented. I shake my head and tell him I just want to chill by myself.

"Dude," Ahmed says, but he doesn't know what else to say. "Come on."

"I'm fine, really. It's no big deal. I'm over it. I just want to hang here. Alone."

I can tell he doesn't want to leave, but he knows I'm not going to change my mind.

"All right, my man, gonna let you off the hook this time, but just this time. Pick you up bright and early," he says. "I'm gonna go work on some new moves, so you better be ready to laugh your ass off tomorrow." He offers me a weak smile that is so un-Ahmed-like that I figure I must be pretty pathetic to look at.

I make myself kind of chuckle, but only because he's trying so hard. I feel guilty that he has to have such a messed-up best friend. He finally leaves, and when I can't stand staring at the ceiling anymore, I order a pizza.

I try to act cool when the delivery guy gets there, but as he stands there trying to make change, I can hardly wait. I nearly take his arm off when I slam the door and head to the couch. I open the box, the warm comforting smell of the dough and sauce acting like a sedative. I take a deep breath and dig in. I start to wonder if eating will be the only thing that will ever make me happy. And maybe I'll eat so much, that one day I'll be one of those guys who has to be rescued by the fire department because he can't fit through the door to get out of his house. And they'll have to rip the roof off and get a crane to lift my fat ass out of here. I choke on the last slice as I picture the whole scene. I run to the bathroom and get rid of it.

Later, when the hunger pang hits me again, I go to bed trying to psyche myself out that the phone will ring. I get up and check to make sure it's working. It is.

But it doesn't ring. Charlotte doesn't call.

• • •

I drag myself out of bed and go to school the next day, but only because Ahmed calls superearly and convinces me that the best thing to do is pretend it didn't bother me at all. I'm tired of pretending, but I crawl into the Roller Skate and go. Ahmed tries to cheer me up. I stare out the window.

I go through the motions of the day, but really, all I care about is Charlotte and whether or not she saw those pictures. If she did, then that's it. Now she knows the real me, and she's probably grossed out that she ever wasted a minute on me.

I sit and wait for her to come through the door during drama, but for the first time that year, she doesn't. She's not in class. I know it's because she can't stand being near me. I know it's because she's embarrassed she ever sort of liked me. But all I can do is think about her, which makes me come up with what's probably the worst idea I've ever had.

I get to Charlotte's house right before eight o'clock. I almost leave when I spot Mark's car, but I had already convinced myself on the walk over that nothing was going to keep me from talking to her tonight. And even as I walk up the stairs and ring the doorbell, I know no good can come of this, but something inside me won't let me turn and run. I need to know. One way or another, I need to know.

She answers the door, but doesn't ask me to come inside. Instead, she comes outside and says, "Charlie, hey, what are you doing here?"

And I'm stumped because I didn't think it out this far. I suddenly wish I'd made note cards because now that I'm here, and she's asking me why I'm here, and she's standing so close, I can't remember. I grasp at the only thing that still connects me to her.

"Um, I missed you in class today." What a stupid thing to say.

"Yeah, I had a follow-up dentist's appointment, so I

left early. I wasn't there yesterday morning, either. One cavity," she says and shrugs her shoulders, but then smiles. She hadn't been there yesterday morning. She hadn't seen the pictures. She didn't know what Mark had done. It made sense. Mark did it when he knew she wouldn't be there because maybe Charlotte would've stopped him or gotten on his case. Though that might be true, I could still make Mark look like a total jerk by telling her about the whole incident. But how could I when it's too embarrassing?

"Oh, okay," I say and think about just leaving it at that and going back home. But I still stand there, and she still stands there, and it feels awkward as hell.

"So, I see you're hanging out with Mark," I say.

"He stopped by, and we decided to watch a movie. You . . . want to join us?" she asks.

Did I want to join them? She definitely didn't know. I wanted to be nowhere near Mark right now, and I wanted him to be nowhere near her. I wanted her to be with me. Just me.

"Nah, it's cool," I say, even though it's not. But I still make no move to leave, so I bring up the exhibit. It's not for a little over a week, and it seems silly that I'm asking her because I know she's going.

"Are you kidding? Of course I'll be there," she says. "I mean, I can't believe there are going to be pictures of me hanging in a gallery." She looks down at the ground. "It made me a little nervous, but it was fun being your muse. Did they turn out okay?" she asks and I feel terrible. What is she going to think when she walks into the gallery and there is no Charlotte

VanderKleaton collection?

"Yeah, of course," I say.

"Good." She breathes a sigh of relief. "My God, Charlie, what if you win?"

I want to crawl into a grave and die. "That'd be cool, I guess," I say because I have no idea what else to say.

"Oh my God, is it snowing?" she says looking past me. I turn to look. She runs out and starts to spin under the falling snowflakes.

It *is* snowing, and I'm here, watching Charlotte VanderKleaton twirl and laugh under the light flurry.

I walk over to where she is and start spinning, too, first slowly, and then faster and faster just like I did when I was a little kid. She does the same, and we keep at it until we fall and crash to the ground, laughing. Suddenly, it's so hard to breath. I stare up at the swirling sky, at the crazy blur of the snow that falls on our faces, and Charlotte tells me about how she loves the snow. . . . God, I wished she loved me.

"So you're going?" I ask Charlotte, still staring up at the sky.

"God, Charlie, YES!" she says and laughs.

I swallow the lump in my throat. Her phone starts ringing in her pocket, she looks down at it and silences it.

"Charlotte?"

"I said yes already!"

"No . . . I mean . . . What is this?" I can't believe I've said it. As soon as I do, I wish I could eat the words right back up, stuff them down, and never let them come out again. But it's too late.

"What?" she asks, even though I can tell by the tone

of her voice that she knows exactly what I mean.

"This, you and me, what is it?" I ask because the words already came out, and I can't take them back. This is the real reason I came over here tonight. I have to know, and Ahmed is right that unless one of us says something, it's just going to keep going on and on like this.

She shrugs. "I guess this is what it is. Do you really, I mean, do we really have to define it? Because I don't know what it is."

I almost say no. I almost let it go. I should just let it go. But I can't.

"I need to know. I need to know something is real. I can't stand the not knowing anymore."

She sits up and faces me.

"I do like you Charlie, really I do, but . . ." She looks down and she looks kind of confused, but I don't care. Because what I feel inside is much worse. I look up at the sky so that she doesn't see my eyes welling up with tears. It's deep and dark and makes me think of the word zenith, and I wish I could get beamed up by some UFO. I am probably the only person willing to be abducted by aliens, willing to let them do whatever to me. I wonder what I look like from way up there. Pathetic?

"You and I, we're different," she says. I barely hear it, but I hear it. And my face flushes with embarrassment. How could I have been so stupid? How could I have ever thought that Charlotte VanderKleaton could ever really like me? It's cold and I'm sure the snowflakes are melting as they hit my burning face, and

I know I should run. I should run and never look back and just forget all the stupid things I let myself believe. But all I can do is lie there and just pray she doesn't say anymore. I think if she explains how she can't be seen with me, I'll . . .

Charlotte looks over at me. "Charlie, do you know why I hate Blanche?" she whispers, and I'm sure I didn't hear her right. How can she be thinking about a stupid play right now? "I hate her," she continues, "because she's fake . . . like me." I'm about to tell her she's out of her mind to compare herself to Blanche, but she goes on.

"Do you know what it's like to never feel like you're enough? Like you're always trying to be something you're not? And when you do that so often, you don't even remember who you really are? I mean, maybe you try to be a certain way for this person, and a certain way for that person, and a totally different way for another person, and everyone is happy. But the problem is, you forget who you really are."

What Charlotte is saying starts confusing me, even as it thunders with some semblance of the deepest shit I've ever heard. I get what she's saying, but I don't know how to be a different person for different people. If I knew, I would stop being the loser that I am for Charlotte.

"What do you mean? Just, you know, be who you are," I say.

"Right. You make it sound so easy, but it's not. Think about it. I mean, are you the person you really are, Charlie? Or do you put up some kind of front?" she asks.

What she says freaks me out because I'm scared Charlotte might have figured out what a big liar I am.

"Charlotte, you're really an amazing person. I can't believe you can't see that." I reach for her hand, but she pulls it away.

"Come on, Charlie, You barely know me. You just think I'm amazing. And the problem with that is that after awhile, you'll see that I'm not."

"No," I say because there's no way Charlotte could be anything but amazing.

"Some people don't know their faults, but I know mine. I'm reminded of them every day." She looks toward her house. "And I know I'm not . . . enough, for you. Besides, Charlie, I don't even really know who you are either. Sometimes I think I do, but then . . ." She sighs deeply and shakes her head like it's too complicated to explain how screwed up I am. My face gets hotter. I wish she'd stop, but she keeps talking. "I get the feeling that there's this part of you that you don't let others see. And if neither of us can be ourselves around each other, then what the hell is the point? We're like two identical puzzle pieces, but two pieces that can never fit."

I don't know if Charlotte is being the sincerest she's ever been or if she's feeding me the biggest load of crap. But I'm pathetic because even as she sits here saying how wrong we are for each other, and even as I want to run away from what she's saying, I can't help thinking she's got it all wrong. We'd be perfect for one another if she'd just give it a chance and stop reading so much into everything.

She looks at me, and there's that thing in her eyes that I tried to get in the pictures and couldn't. Part of me does understand what she's saying, but then I don't see how telling her all about my fat self and my crazy mom and my shitty dad will make any difference.

"Say something," she says. But I can't. I want to tell her I love her and that I don't want her to ever leave me. But I think if I say those things, she'll just dismiss it because somehow it's wrong for me to think she's amazing. So I say nothing. All I can do is lie in the snow and let her tell me she can't be with me because this, being left, is what I know.

"Don't be mad, Charlie, please. I do care about you. I just, I mean, look what happened with Blanche and Mitch." I can tell she's struggling, but I don't care because I feel like an idiot and like I've been given the Rubik's Cube of break-up speeches.

"Do you . . . are you together with him?" I ask because I figure I might as well plunge this knife in as deep as it will go.

She sighs. "I don't know. I mean he's . . ." She shrugs her shoulders. "I know where I stand with him. I don't have to try so hard with him, and at least he's real with me. He is who he is, whether people like it or not," she says finally.

I hate that she's making Mark sound so noble. Who cares if Mark is real because he's a big dumbass? I want to tell her this and that I'll accept who she is, and I can't imagine her being anything but perfect, but I know she's not and that's okay. I want to beg her not to leave me because I'm suddenly aware these will be my last moments alone with Charlotte, and however miserable and confusing they might be, I don't want them to end. I just want somebody here. I need some-body to stay with me.

"Charlie," she says as she leans over, kisses my cheek, and rests her forehead on my temple. "I'm sorry. I wish things could be different."

She gets up and heads back into her house. The door creaks as she opens and closes it, and I stay on the ground. I want to run after her and tell her I'll do any-thing if only she'll stay, if only she'll love me back and let me love her. But I don't.

I get up and walk home. I go through the neighbor-hood and picture everyone put away in their little compartments, and I can't help but wonder if the pret-tiest compartments are the ones trying to cover up the ugliest messes inside. I wonder what it would be like to be invisible and walk through all the compartments on the block. I wonder how many people would be locked in little rooms, hiding away.

When I get home, Dad is actually there but on the phone in his office. I don't know if I remembered to get rid of the pizza box. But I don't care anymore. I trudge upstairs, pass Mom's bedroom door, and close it. It's easier to pretend she's still here when the door is closed. It's easier to pretend that nobody's left me.

PART THREE
BLUR

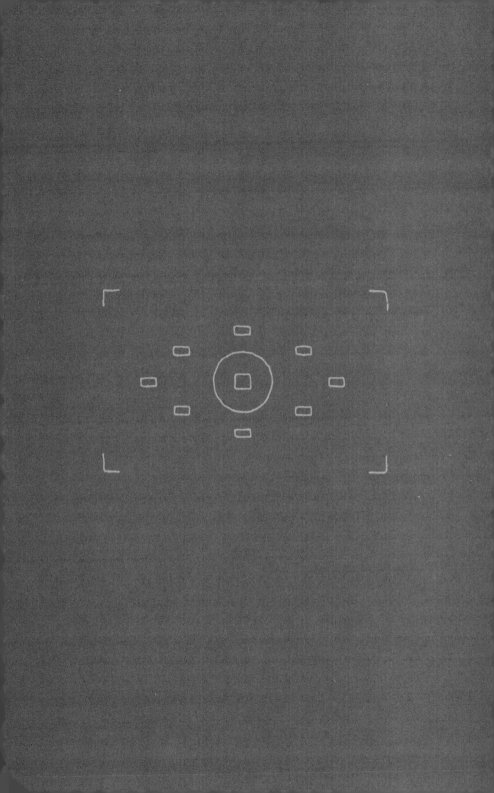

CHAPTER SEVENTEEN

Here's what I know:

People aren't who you think they are.

Things don't always work out the way you expected them to.

Sometimes . . . we miss things.

Here's what I don't know:

What I'm still missing.

•••

I feel like I should be seeing something that I can't see. Like I'm missing the signs or the connectors. They're floating around right in front of me, *right in front of me*, but they're invisible or maybe they're too close. But pretty soon that last piece is going to click into place, and I'm going to step back and think, I should've known. But by then, it might be too late.

I skip school the next day. Ahmed does too and we hang at my house, watching stupid shows on TV. When Dad gets home, he brings dinner. A couple of veggie subs. Ahmed and I take them up to my room, even though Dad looks a little disappointed that we don't hang out with him.

Ahmed is in the middle of telling me how he makes sure to hog up most of his locker between classes because then when Janie bends over him to get her books, he gets a good view down her shirt.

"Today's view was particularly AMAZING, brother! I mean, sure there was Tina," he says as he rolls his eyes and dismisses the memory of her, "but these babies . . . wow!" He shakes his head and takes a bite of his sub.

"Right," I say, still depressed about the whole thing with Charlotte last night.

"Okay, I know you're bummed. But just think of all the chickies out there that you have yet to meet. Come on, she's cute and all, but think about it. College is right around the corner, and you don't want to be tied down in some serious high school relationship. Haven't you watched those movies with college girls in them? They're in a whole different league, you know? No more of this little teasing shit. That's the real thing." He starts pumping his hips in the air. "Oh, just like that."

"Dude, I really don't want to watch you air hump right now, or ever," I tell him.

"All right." He puts his sub down and throws himself on my bed. "This better?" he yells as he pumps his hips on my bed. He flops around and starts yelling, "Janie, Janie!"

"Shut up, man. And quit doing that on my bed!"

He laughs and sits up. "Laugh, dude, it's not the end of the world."

"Dude, just stop, all right?" I say because I don't feel like being cheered up and I don't feel like pretending that I'm amused by Ahmed's antics right now. I take another bite of my sandwich. The girl of my dreams just told me we can never be and still, I have no problem eating. It figures.

"Fine," he says, and I know he's irritated but I don't feel like apologizing.

The phone rings and my stomach drops as I wonder if maybe Charlotte has had a change of heart. A few minutes later, I hear Dad's footsteps, and he cracks open the door to my room.

"Charlie?" he says.

My God, it's her! Maybe she had time to think about it. Maybe she stayed up all night thinking about how much she really does want to give me another chance.

"I got it, Dad!" I jump up and start to head out of the room.

"Charlie." Dad is in the way and doesn't move as I try to get past him.

"Watch out, Dad," I say, hoping she doesn't hang up.

"Charlie, it's not for you." My stomach drops. It wasn't Charlotte. But the heavy feeling in my stomach stays because even in that millisecond before he speaks, I know whatever's coming has to do with Mom.

"Listen, Charlie," Dad says. He takes a deep breath. "I . . . have to go get Mom." His voice cracks.

I don't have the nerve ask him what the hell that means. Ahmed drops the last bit of his sub and scrambles to pick it up. Nobody says anything, and for a minute I think maybe Dad didn't really say it. He must think the same thing because he says it again.

"I have to go get Mom," he says again but more slowly.

The way he says it scares the shit out of me, like she's in a body bag and she's incapable of coming home herself, or if we don't get her she'll disappear forever and maybe she won't have ever existed in the first place.

"Where is she?" I ask.

"Florida." He looks like he wants to say more, but he doesn't and turns to leave.

"I'm going," I say. Both he and Ahmed look at me as I grab a bag and start shoving some clothes in it. He shakes his head, but I just say "I'm going" more firmly. He knows I've made up my mind and even if he doesn't like it, I don't think he's in the mood to put up a fight.

He nods. "I'll make the flight arrangements."

• • •

During the drive to the airport, I finally ask him what I've been wanting to ask him because I can't keep guessing anymore.

"Is she alive?" I mutter. I don't want to know, but I have to know. He doesn't flinch when I ask him; he's not even taken by surprise. He must have thought about it already.

"Yes," he says, "she's alive." His voice is flat, and I wonder if she really is.

I have a thousand questions, but I'm not ready for all the answers yet. We say nothing more the rest of the ride. I don't want to think of how Mom is broken; how she's cracked and shattered and now we're on our way to pick up little pieces of her.

It's still dark outside. The snow that fell last night

has turned into a slushy gray mess. Was it just last night that it snowed, that it was pure and white and falling? Was it just last night that Charlotte was in front of her house, twirling in front of me? How we were in our fake little world. I remember her cold kiss on my cheek. And then, how I went home to my house, and upstairs to my little compartment and Dad was in his little compartment. Mom's little compartment down the hall was empty, again. And we didn't care. It's strange, how we seal ourselves in. We can be right next to each other and not hear anything. We just look up and wait for snow, a smile, or a fracture, afraid of screaming for help, afraid of tearing down walls. Except Mom. Mom had been screaming and banging on the walls all this time. But we ignored her.

Dad and I rush to catch our flight and barely make it. I don't notice anyone or anything, and I'm glad the loud hum of the plane's engine almost shuts out the thoughts in my head. And I don't know how we can be landing when we only just left, but we are and there's noise and other people as we get off, but I feel like my ears are stuffed, their voices muffled and far away.

Soon, we're driving a rental car, listening to the fake politeness of the GPS person.

"Charlie," Dad starts, "the call was from a motel clerk where your Mom has been staying for a while. He said she was in really bad shape and someone needed to come and get her." He says it so robotically that for a minute I think his words came out of the GPS. I let this sink in for a moment.

"How long has she been there?"

He takes a deep breath and sighs before answering, "Over a month."

I think of how I saw Dad track down Mom one time and found out she was in Maine by tracking her credit card purchases.

"Did you know?"

I look over at Dad. He keeps his eyes on the road in front of him and doesn't say anything.

"Did you know?" I demand.

He nods.

"After everything, you didn't . . . ?"

"I thought she needed time. I thought she'd be okay. I didn't know what to do. She's always been okay."

I shake my head in disbelief.

"Don't," he says, "I just . . ." He searches for words, but there are none.

"How bad is she?" I ask him. He's silent, "Dad, how bad?" I demand. I look over and he starts shaking his head. "I don't know," he manages finally. The uncertainty of the words mixes with the stifling artificial heat of the car and makes it hard to breath.

We arrive at the motel and Dad pretends our headlights didn't just flicker over a prostitute leaning into the window of some rusty old car as we turn into a noname motel. She looks over at us with lazy eyes, before turning her attention back to the shadow in the car.

Two guys sit outside the entrance of the motel, arguing. They look at Dad, who even in his disheveled clothing, even with his grave face, is notably out of place. They size him up, but he doesn't look their way as we enter the motel office. It smells like mildew. The guy behind the counter is old, and he squints at us as we approach the desk.

"Hi, uh . . . are you Jim?" Dad asks.

"Uh-huh," the old man says. "Who's asking?"

"You called me about my wife."

"Oh, right. Yeah, she's been holed up in that room for a couple weeks now. She's caused a fuss ya know, yelling at people for no reason, screamin'. I tried talkin' to her, but she just yelled and cried and carried on. But, she always ended up going back to her room so . . ." The old man squints at me and back at Dad. "Anyway, caught some good-for-nothin' tryin' to break into her room the other night, so I figures I'd try to track someone down. When she came here, didn't look like she was from here, ya know what I mean?" He looks at Dad and he nods his head. "Besides, her credit card run out, ain't workin' anymore, and I ain't runnin' no shelter here, so you gonna have to take care of this first." He shoves a bill in Dad's face. "And best to get rollin' outta here soon." He keeps looking over at me and squinting. I don't think he has teeth, but it's hard to tell through the dirty gray beard covering his face. "Room seven," he says after Dad pays. He throws a key in Dad's direction and turns back to an old TV where a show is desperately fighting through the static.

We pass the same guys on the way out, and I wonder if it was one of them that tried to break into Mom's room. We walk quickly and I hope to God they don't follow us.

Five seconds later we're in front of a door with a crooked seven on the front. Dad doesn't seem to contemplate what's on the other side like I do. He just knocks and calls out, "Carmen, it's Doug." Maybe he does this so she doesn't get startled, maybe he half expects her to open the door with a smile and a kiss. I don't know, but it seems weird and I almost laugh, which makes me think I must be like the biggest freak on the planet. I don't know how you can feel like laughing and screaming at the same time, but you can.

Dad looks at me and I swallow the crazy laughter that threatens to explode out of me. He puts the key in the keyhole, turns the knob, and opens the door.

I'm not sure what I expected. I guess nothing would have surprised me. If Mom had actually opened the door with a smile and a kiss, maybe it would have seemed oddly normal. If she lay broken in a million pieces, scattered over the dingy motel carpet, maybe I would have just started sweeping her up. I don't know. I was ready for anything, which is why when I see that the room is empty, I'm surprised, but not. She's not here. And I'm worried, and I just want to see her. I have to tell her I'm sorry and that I get it, or that I'm starting to get it. But we have flown all the way here, navigated through Satan's fucking garden, and arrived at the front of crooked number seven's door only to find she's not here.

"Where is she?" I whisper.

Dad walks in first. Only the faint light from the bathroom illuminates the dark room. I walk in behind him and the smell of sweat, piss, mold, and old food hits me immediately. Was she really staying here? Is this really where she chose to hide? How could anyone in his or her right mind stay in a place like this?

The place would be disgusting even without the

scattered take-out containers on the bed, floor, and night table, but the addition of it definitely made it worse. The bed has some clothes piled on it that I think might be Mom's but I'm not sure.

"This is it," Dad says, even though I see him glancing at the number on the door that we left open. "If not, the key wouldn't work." He runs his hand through his hair. "What the fuck?" he says, shaking his head as he takes the place in. I've never seen him so completely awestruck. I didn't know he was really capable of being shocked, not after all the crap we'd been through with Mom.

"Should we wait?" I ask.

He shrugs his shoulders. "Yeah, I guess, but will she come back?" he asks.

I look around and spot her purse on the floor next to the bed. "Her purse is here," I say, gesturing to it.

Dad picks it up. "Wallet, too." He starts taking out different items and throwing them on the bed; keys, cinnamon gum, a ton of receipts, a book.

I pick up the book and study the cover. It's old and beat up. It says: *Crossing the Water* by Sylvia Plath.

"I didn't know Mom liked poetry," I say.

"Yeah, she did. When we were in college, she got a poem published in the university magazine. She never wrote anything more after that, so I thought she just, you know . . ." He looks up at me and shrugs his shoulders, and I know exactly what he means. Somewhere in our attic were half-finished mosaic tables, warped pottery, badly knit beginnings of what were meant to be scarves or sweaters. All had started out with Mom's usual over-the-top enthusiasm only to be forgotten a few days later.

I start looking through the book as Dad pulls out more receipts. It's riddled with notes written in the margins, most of which I can't make out. The writing kind of scares me, though. It seems frantic and rambling and there are exclamation points screaming off the pages and several words viciously underlined, some causing small rips. I run my hands over the pages, over Mom's writing, over a poem titled, *Mirror*, that was earmarked. This must have been the last one she was reading.

"Dad?" I say and work up the nerve to ask what I'm not really sure I want to know the answer to. "Do you think Mom will be okay?"

He takes a deep breath, closes his eyes, and rubs his forehead.

"Yeah, she'll . . ." He looks at me and then stops. We're both struck; we've crossed some invisible line. We've never been here before. We can't go back. He shakes his head and lets out a long sigh.

"Honestly, Charlie? I don't know," he says. "I have no idea if she's going to be all right." The honesty catches me off guard. Him too, I think. He searches for what to say next. "I know I've been a jerk . . ." He looks down at the floor. "But I'm going to be there for her from now on, for both of you. I promise. I don't know how I let everything get so bad." He shakes his head. He looks lost. I've been wanting him to feel bad. I've been wanting him to say it's all his fault. To let him feel like shit for a change. But now that he does, and is admitting to me that he's been wrong all along, I don't know if it's what I ever really wanted.

I shrug. Maybe he wants me to say something that will make it all not his fault. I wish I could give him that, but if I say it's not his fault, I know I won't really mean it. And if I say that it is his fault, I know I won't mean that, either. So I don't say anything, because nothing is truly black and white. There are so many shades of gray.

"I've known she's needed help, and I didn't . . ." He stares at her purse in his hands. "I mean, I hope she'll be fine, but I, I don't know if she will be." Those last words clip the air. They sound too final, too ominous. He realizes it and quickly tries to fill the hanging silence.

"I mean, she'll . . . we'll get her help . . . just as soon as we find her." He looks down. He doesn't say anything for a long time.

"Yeah," I say because it's all that comes out.

The knock at the half-open door startles both of us. It's Jim from the lobby.

"Sorry to interrupt," he starts, "but a couple a' fellas said they think your lady saw y'all and slipped out right before y'all came in here."

"Yeah, looks like she's gone," Dad mutters.

"It's not really my business, but, well, I've seen her wander around here sometimes late at night, so maybe she's still around here, waiting to see if you leave." He smacks his lips. I know he's trying to be nice, but I'm suddenly bothered that this old man knows more about Mom than I do. And I hate that he's probably right— Mom would be waiting for us to leave.

"Let's go look for her," I tell Dad. He nods and we head outside.

It's not really cold outside, but just enough for me to see my breath as I start jogging around the motel, looking for Mom. Dad heads in the opposite direction. The old man limps behind me, his hands in the pockets of his overalls, and I start to wonder if maybe he's not as nice as he seems. What if this was some kind of trap? What if he was trying to split up Dad and me? The two guys that were sitting outside could be attacking Dad right now. They could've done something to Mom and just lured us here to rob us or something. I speed up. The old man keeps up, too.

I don't know if I should call out for Mom or not. Maybe she needed my help. Or maybe she was hiding from us. I listen, but don't hear Dad calling for her either. I don't know if that's good or bad.

The motel is like a maze and everything I pass looks exactly the same. The same paint-chipped doors, the same eerie balconies. Balconies. Maybe she'd gone up to the second level where she would have a good view of us leaving. I race up the stairs, the old man shuffling behind me. I run around to what seems like the back of the motel and look down.

The view below is dark with only dim bulbs outside each room serving as light, making it hard to see. But I can make out what looks like a pool in the motel's back patio, and it strikes me as odd that such a rundown fleabag place like this should have a pool. It's dark and only the reflection of the moon on the water let's me know it's there.

The old man comes up right next to me, and he squints in the same direction. "Jesus Christ, son . . . ," he whispers and starts half limping, half running, back to the way we came. "Somebody call an ambulance! Somebody call a god-damn ambulance!"

I look frantically in the direction he was looking in, and I know I should be moving, running, and yelling, but I can't. Not until I see what he saw. And then I do. There's a limp, dark figure floating on the surface of the pool. Mom.

I run and head down the stairs, screaming and yelling. I run past the old man.

"Mom! Dad! Mom!"

"Charlie!" I can hear Dad's voice in the distance somewhere and the voices of other men. Some doors creak open as I pass, as I try to figure out how the hell to get back there.

"Dad! The pool! She's in the pool!" I yell in a voice that I don't even recognize as my own. I run faster, hoping it's not too late. I round a corner and finally see the pool ahead, and Dad finally comes from the other side, and then he jumps into the pool. But it's all happening slowly now.

"Carmen!" Dad yells. "Carmen!" The two other men who were outside when we first arrived at the motel come to the edge of the pool, yelling directions, grabbing at the giant, ragged leaf in the pool that Dad is trying to get to safety. I try to run over to him but fall and crash onto the concrete. My face scrapes across the ground, but I don't feel anything. I scramble to get up and race over to help and jump in.

The water is freezing, and we pull and push, but she doesn't move. The big green sweater she's wearing wants to swallow her whole. Her face is an eerie pale color; the light of the moon giving everything a surreal hue. I'm scared. I'm scared of her being dead.

We finally get her out of the pool. Dad pulls himself out. Someone is screaming and sobbing. Dad is counting, pressing Mom's chest. I feel like someone is punching my chest. Who is crying? I think it could be me. What's been in the pit of my stomach all this time comes rushing out. All my screams have now escaped; they rush out and flood me. I watch Dad kiss Mom and breathe life into her tired body. Then he presses her chest and counts again. Somewhere else a siren blares. But it's all too slow. The old man's face floats in front of me; he's talking to me, but I don't understand words anymore. I think I'm underwater. All I hear are gurgles.

There are more hands, hands pushing Dad out of the way, hands under my arms, hands pulling me up and dragging me out of the way, hands on Mom, people around her. Dad next to me. His chest heaving, waiting, for a sign. We wait. I can't breath. The gurgling is too loud.

"We have vitals," someone yells. Dad crumbles.

"Let's move," someone else says.

They take her away.

CHAPTER EIGHTEEN

My sneakers squeak on the hospital floor as we come in. Dad is frantic and demands to know what's going on with her. A nurse tries to calm him down, but he won't, so she shoves him into a seat and tells him to wait and she'll go find out. I sit next to him. I'm still wet. Dad is still wet. Mom just tried to drown herself. Mom just tried to kill herself. This kind of stuff doesn't really happen, does it? I think back to the last time I was in the hospital for Mom. I think of how scared I was as I watched the doctor hand Mom over to Mr. Killinger like she might break. I think of how this is the second time I've raced to a hospital for Mom. Yes. This kind of stuff is really happening.

Nurses glance up at us, and one comes over and hands Dad a clipboard. They speak in subdued voices. A doctor comes through a pair of swinging doors.

He quickly introduces himself, before telling us the only thing that matters. "She's stable," he says, "the CPR you administered probably saved her from being deprived of oxygen too long. She's not quite coherent, and we have to run tests to check for any further complications." He chooses his next words carefully. "The medics on the scene explained this was nonaccidental?" He looks to Dad for confirmation of what he already knows.

"No, not accidental," Dad mutters. The doctor nods his head.

"I think you should know we had to pump her stomach, too. She took a large dose of aspirin in addition to . . ." He hesitates and looks at me before looking back at Dad. "I'm sorry. I'll send our social service coordinator over to talk to you in just a minute. She can give you more information. I'll update you regularly, but as of now, I can tell you for sure that she'll have to stay for observation," he says.

"Can we see her?" I ask.

"I'll send a nurse to get you as soon as that's possible," he answers. "In the meantime, I'll have Ms. McKnight come out and speak with you." He pats Dad on the shoulder, and goes back through the swinging doors.

A woman in regular clothes with a hospital employee badge comes out after a period of time and takes Dad to a room. She won't let me go with them. I wait. Sick and broken people come in. Sick and broken people leave. The clock ticks. I wait. I wonder where Mom is waiting. The ceiling is a bunch of cork tiles. The floor is dull and scuffed. The nurses eat chips. I imagine eating too. I imagine throwing up. I picture the chunks floating in the toilet. I'm hypnotized by the chunks, by the water with gray ribbons that strangle mom. I think hours go by. I think part of me is still on the concrete back at the motel. I look at the cork ceiling again. The scuffed floor. The sick and broken people that come in. I can't let my mind go back to the dark places where Mom was. I can't let it go to that pool. A nurse comes over and cleans my face.

Finally Dad comes back and takes me to see Mom. I gasp for air. He knows where to turn, what room to go into. He's seen her already. He stops suddenly.

"Charlie?" he turns to look at me and takes a deep breath. I know he's trying to prepare me somehow.

"Dad, I know." I don't know what I know . . . but I know what this is like. He nods.

"Okay," he says, more to himself than to me, and starts walking again. He points to let me know she's in room 216. I stop outside the door and try to take a deep breath. My hands shake. I cross my arms across my chest to stop them, brace myself, and walk in.

Mom looks slight, even on the small hospital bed, barely noticeable under the thin white sheets. She's facing the closed windows. I want to cry. I want to sit on the floor, where she can't see me, and cry until all of this goes away.

I clear my throat, "Mom?"

She doesn't stir or look my way. Dad walks around to the other side of the bed and bends down so his face is level with hers. He takes one of her hands in his.

"Carmen? Charlie's here," he whispers. I walk around next to Dad.

Mom's pale face stares back at me, her eyes dark and dull and flat, like two buttonholes on a limp rag doll. There's a mottled bruise on the side of her face that goes from her cheek down to her jaw. I don't know how she could have gotten that, and even though she almost died, it's this bruise that I can hardly handle. I swallow the lump creeping up my throat. Dad looks over at me to see if I'm all right. I'm not, but I bite down hard and set my face in what I hope looks like strength.

"You okay?" he asks.

I nod, not trusting my voice, afraid if I say something there might be one last scream that escapes me, and I'll be stuck with it forever ringing in my ears. I'm too scared to touch her. I don't know what to do with myself.

"Need to go outside?"

I shake my head. I don't want to see her like this, but I can't leave her.

I pull the chair next to the bed closer and sit down. I can't stand anymore. I lay my head down on the bed and close my eyes. Dad sits on the chair on the other side of the room. I'm relieved, I don't want him to see the tears rolling down my face. If we had loved her enough, she would have stayed. We would have been enough, and she wouldn't have to escape to strange motels, to dark, dangerous, bottomless places where she wanted to die. I open my eyes, escaping images I don't want to relive. I focus on the quiet TV. Sports announcers are laughing. The world doesn't make sense. Everyone should stop. How can they laugh? My head hurts from plugging up my tears. The sports announcers keep laughing.

Something light lands on my head. Mom's hand, weak and fluttery, like a small bird landed on me. I don't move, not an inch, so it won't be scared away. It flutters around. I reach up and hold it. I hold the cold broken bird, make it warm, and close my eyes again.

• • •

I wake up with a cramp in my neck and with Mom's hand still in mine. I turn and look at her. Her eyes are closed and she doesn't stir.

"Mom?" I whisper, but she doesn't move. I touch her arm. "Mom," I say louder, "wake up." I want to see her alive.

She moves, and I keep calling her, trying to get her back, pulling that rope that will bring her back to us. She opens her button eyes. Empty.

"Mom . . ."

"Charlie?" she murmurs.

"I'm here. We're here." She nods. "We're here," I tell her. "You're not alone, Mom. Not anymore."

She nods. And looks at the ceiling.

"Mom?" she blinks. "Mom?" She won't look at me. "Please look at me." Tears roll out of the corner of her eyes.

Dad comes in with three cups of coffee.

"Thought you might want some," he says to me, and then looks at Mom. "Carmen," he says, and I'm amazed how her name, that he's said a million times, can come out like that, like a breath.

He walks over to Mom and leans down next to her. "Coffee?" he whispers. She doesn't respond, but he sets it down in front of her and kisses her cheek. She winces. He jerks back and quickly tries to wipe away the hurt written on his face.

She looks at the white paper cup, then to Dad, then to me. She looks startled, like we just appeared out of nowhere. It's like she's never seen us before.

"You're here," she says.

"Yeah," Dad says.

"Why?" she whispers, fresh tears making her blank eyes glisten. I look over at Dad and say, "Because we love you." And then he starts sobbing uncontrollably and tells her he's sorry, and she's weeping, too. I feel more screams gurgle up and out of my throat, but instead they're choking sounds and tears. And we cry and hold on to each other because we're really all we can hold on to anymore. All along we've been flailing and thrashing and barely treading water, and if we don't hold on to each other, we'll never make it. We'll end up sinking to the bottom and then float lifelessly to the top.

• • •

While they run some more tests on Mom, Ms. McKnight comes back and asks to speak to Dad and me. She leads both of us to a room with chairs and boxes of tissues. Some small tables are scattered with magazines and a TV is mounted to the wall in the corner. I wonder how many people have waited here or how many other kids have sat here after their moms tried to kill themselves.

I try to pay attention to what Ms. McKnight says, but my ears still don't quite work. Everything comes through like I have water in them. Words sound muffled, deep, and far away. She drills Dad with questions. Ms. McKnight is short and thin, and wears a fixed frown on her face. She asks about Mom's history and how long she's displayed this kind of behavior. Dad slumps further into himself, and from somewhere that sounds far away, I hear him say that Mom has always

kind of been this way but that she had gotten worse little by little over the years. I concentrate harder and
their conversation becomes clearer. She suggests that
upon our return home, we put Mom in a facility where
she can get the appropriate evaluations and help she
needs. Her suggestions are more like demands. She
hands some papers to Dad and goes on about the long
term effects of this on the whole family, eyes me specifically, and goes on to discuss the absolute necessity of
family therapy.

"It's not his fault," I tell her, a little tired of Ms.
McKnight. I look at Dad and say what I couldn't before,
"It's not your fault." He bites his lip and looks down.

"It's nobody's fault," Ms. McKnight says, her frozen
face thawing slightly, "but you still have to deal with it
the right way. You have to be willing to acknowledge
it." She takes the edge out of her voice.

"Your Mom does need help, Charlie. And even if you
might not think it, you and your father need help, too.
Things can only get better that way. You want things to
get better, don't you?"

"Yeah," I tell her, wondering if it's really possible,
and so wanting to believe her.

• • •

While we wait for final test results, Dad gets our stuff
from the car so we can change our clothes. We both
realize Mom will need fresh clothes, too, for when she
leaves. Dad says he'll go get them but instead returns
an hour later with jogging pants and a T-shirt with

price tags on them. It occurs to me that Dad isn't planning on going back to the motel room. I catch Dad outside Mom's hospital room.

"What about all her stuff?" I say, an image of her things scattered about some strange, dark room flashes through my mind.

"We have her purse and wallet. Jim from the motel brought it by last night after you fell asleep," he says.

"Really?" The old man's face floats in front of me again. "What about everything else?"

Dad takes a deep breath. "Any other stuff can be replaced," he says. "We have her. That's all we need. Anyway, I can't go back there."

"Right," I mumble. The image of the motel room where Mom had been living goes through my head again. And Mom floating on the surface of the pool. "Sorry for bringing it up."

"No, God, Charlie. Please don't apologize to me, never again. I'm the one who is sorry. I am sorry, Charlie. And we will talk about all of this. We can't just go on pretending. There's a lot we have to work through." He gives me a hard hug.

"Dad?" I have to tell him. If I don't tell him now, I might never tell him. I'll go on pretending.

"Yeah, Charlie?"

I look down at the floor. "I gotta tell you something."

He looks at me, searches my eyes for some clue of what I'm about to lay on him. I take a deep breath.

"Dad, I . . ." How do I say it? "Um . . ." He waits. "Dad . . . I . . ." I look down at my shoes. There's only one way to say it. "I throw up." His face goes from uncertainty to confusion. Holy shit, I can't believe I said it.

"What do you mean? Are you sick?"

"No, I mean . . ." How do I explain this? "I throw up. When I eat too much. I eat a lot. Not all the time, but, sometimes I try not to eat at all and then I can't take it anymore and . . ." I think he realizes what I'm saying. "Then I eat everything and then I just, I . . . get rid of it."

"Charlie." It comes out slow and quiet, the way he said Mom's name. I look at Dad's fallen face, his hunched over shoulders; I just let out the last bit of air in him.

"I'm sorry," I say. I'm sweaty from the heat and shame that has risen up my back and pooled in my face. Dad doesn't say anything. For a minute, I think he's going to yell at me, but he grabs me by the shoulders.

"Don't apologize," he says, digging his fingers into my shirt. "Never apologize to me again. I'm the one who's sorry, for every stupid thing I've done, for making you feel this way, for putting too much pressure on you. Don't you ever be sorry. None of this, none of it, is your fault, okay?" I don't answer him because I'm not sure I believe him.

"Okay?" he says. He shakes me, hard. "Okay?" he insists.

I'm frozen. He's wrong. It is my fault.

"Charlie, none of this is your fault," he repeats. "You have to know that, please." He squeezes my shoulders harder and harder with each word. I wonder if he could break my bones if I don't answer. "Please?"

I nod. "Okay," I say finally because his eyes are red

and bloodshot, because his face is sagging with guilt, because he looks the worst I've ever seen him. But I'm still not sure I believe him.

"I love you, Charlie," he says, not letting go of my shoulders. "I love you."

"Me too, Dad."

He hugs me. When he doesn't let go, I tell him we should get back to Mom.

"Yeah, okay, go ahead." His grip eases up and finally, he lets go. "I'll be there in a minute." He puts his head in his hands, and I go back into Mom's room, trying not to think about the look on Dad's face.

•••

Dad decides it'd be better not to fly home, so he arranges for us to drive back in the rental car. I'm glad. I'd been worried about getting on a plane with Mom. What if she freaked out while we were thousands of miles in the air, with nowhere to go? Images of Mom opening the door and jumping out of the plane had been flooding my mind. Driving was definitely a better choice.

The doctors say it's okay to go and they discharge Mom. *Sick and broken people leave.* We walk out of the hospital, to a strange world in a strange place and we have to find our way home.

I feel like we've been living in the same day, but everyone else has kept going. The past and the future don't exist. I can't remember yesterday. Was yesterday the day I saw Mom's limp body floating in the pool? I don't know anymore. Days, weeks, years have gone by since then.

I don't know how Dad is awake. I don't know how he drives without blinking. We stop only for gas, bathroom breaks, and once for food. Dad steals sideways glances at me as we drive and eat, no doubt wondering if I'm going to throw up in the take-out bag. I don't, but I want to because it always makes me feel better. Even if it leaves me feeling empty.

Mom barely makes a sound the whole drive home. We never leave her alone. We go to the bathroom in turns. She barely moves. Dad put her in the backseat when we left the hospital. At first I thought it was because he wanted her to be able to lie down and sleep if she wanted to, but then I caught him clicking the child safety locks, and every time we got in or out of the car, he made sure to hit the automatic lock button.

I'm awake when we drive into our town. It's dreary, or maybe it just looks that way because it's so early in the morning. There's no traffic on the streets, and everything is eerily still, everyone and everything still sleeping. It all looks familiar, but at the same time everything feels different, like I've been gone for a really long time.

We pull into our driveway and Dad wakes up Mom, who starts crying when she sees our house. I can't tell if it's because she's happy to be back home or because she'd rather be anywhere but here. Maybe it's both. I can't decide either.

Our house is dark and cold when we get inside, and I get this crazy urge to yell at the top of my lungs because it seems so empty. All I want to do is fill it up with something.

Dad takes Mom upstairs to their room and puts her in bed. We both sit down on the bed with her. What do we do now? Dad takes a deep breath and tells Mom—us—that we're going to get some help. Mom doesn't say anything, but at least she's there. Her eyes register understanding and I think . . . maybe, relief. Then we all stay put for a long time. I lie down at the foot of the bed and stare at the ceiling and hear the unmistakable hiss of a school bus. I wonder what day it is, and wait for what we do next. Find help.

CHAPTER NINETEEN

Help—it turns out—is Mom going to some sort of facility called New Day Treatment Center. I don't exactly know what it treats, and when we make the two-hour drive a day later to take Mom there, I keep looking around wondering if everyone I see is crazy. The staff is dressed in regular clothing, not white scrubs or anything like that, but they do wear cards around their neck that they slide through black slots on the walls to open doors. Besides that, it seems like a nice place, and the people who work there all have nice smiles and kind eyes that make you feel choked up.

Mom's room is small, and the walls are a buttery yellow that feels like you're in someone's living room. It's nice and I'm glad it's not blue or green or some other color that's supposed to be calming but is really just very cold and hospital-y. There are two beds, but Mom doesn't seem to have a roommate. That seems funny to me, Mom having a roommate, but then I feel bad that Mom might have to share a room with some stranger.

A lady comes in and tells us we can visit for an hour and walk around the facility even, but then we have to leave. Dad looks at her and nods, and Mom fidgets nervously with her hair. My parents suddenly strike me as very clueless, and it seems weird to me that they should have to listen to this woman, that they need direction and they don't really know what to do. My parents have never been those perfect parents, but it's weird that they are still so human and messed up.

We follow the suggestion of the lady—whose name is Kelly, the program facilitator—and go outside for a walk. It's cold and gray and although there are a lot of trees along the path, they are bare with long leafless branches. I'm glad when Kelly comes to the family area an hour later where the three of us are sitting, and gently tells us it's time to go. Mom and Dad hug for a long time, and I suddenly realize that despite all the incredible crap we've been through, they still actually love each other. Then it's my turn, and there's so much I want to say to her like I'll miss you and we'll be back and we're not leaving you. I want her to understand we're not leaving her. But for now all I can manage is *love you* as I hold her tight. And then Kelly is leading Mom down the hall, and we watch her go.

When Dad asks the girl at the front desk for information on therapists in our area, I'm relieved. Maybe you're not supposed to want to talk to a therapist and maybe I'm weird because I do, but I just want to tell someone about all this crazy stuff in my head and get it out. I want to tell someone who doesn't know me and who won't sit there feeling sorry for me. Who knows, maybe it will suck, and maybe there's a reason why most people get uneasy around therapists. But I hope it doesn't because I think I'm ready to stop bottling up everything and carrying it around with me.

The girl gives Dad some business cards, which Dad tucks carefully into his wallet. He looks over at me and says, "Good."

And I think, yes, this is good.

PART FOUR
FIELD OF VIEW

CHAPTER TWENTY

Here's what I know:

Things can get worse before they can get better.

The Universe has really had it out for me.

One thing can have the potential to change your life forever.

Here's what I don't know:

What's coming next.

• • •

I haven't been to school in a week. It's wild. I feel like I haven't been back in years. Dad spoke with Ms. Sheldon about what happened, and she apparently told my teachers so they wouldn't go and yell at me about not doing my schoolwork. Some pretend like nothing's happened and treat me the same. Then there's Ms. Stephen, my sociology teacher, who is old and looks like she wants to take me home and bake me a cake. She gives me a little pat on the shoulder when I come to class and looks at the scrape on my face with genuine concern from when I fell. I don't mind. It's kind of nice. Then there's Mr. Killinger. He asks me to stay after class.

"You should've told me," he says once the last student has left.

"I know," I say.

"I could've helped. I told you to talk to me whenever."

"Yeah, I know, but . . ." My voice trails off. I shrug my shoulders.

"Yeah," he says, "I know. But, you gotta know when to ask for help. I mean, that's a lot to deal with, Charlie." He looks really concerned, and I feel bad that I didn't talk to him. "We talk, regularly, from now on. Okay?"

I nod. "Okay."

"All right, so long as we're clear." He looks around and changes the subject to spare me the lecture. "So, you ready for the exhibit on Friday?"

I shrug my shoulders. "I guess."

"Well, I know you don't really need this now, but Dr. Hoyt wants all of you to have some kind of speech prepared in case you win."

"That sucks," I say.

"I know." He laughs, and I laugh, and laughing feels sort of good again.

I go to lunch and Ahmed is telling me about how Samantha Kineski, who we've known since the sixth grade, got her nose pierced while I was gone, and now she has this huge earring in her nose that he finds oddly attractive. But I'm only half listening because I notice Tanya sitting in the corner of the cafeteria eating a bagged lunch and reading some kind of fantasy novel by herself. And I know it's because of all the stuff with Mom and maybe it'll blow up in my face, but I kind of want to, I don't know, not see Tanya shoved in that corner alone anymore.

"You ready to commit high school suicide?" I ask Ahmed. His eyes go wide at the word suicide since he knows everything that went down and I realize my poor choice of words.

"I mean, do you care about being branded a social misfit for the remainder of our high school career?"

"Dude, look at me," he says, and I laugh at this as I take in Ahmed's latest purple blazer and matching wing tips. I have no idea where he got purple wing tips, but he's got them.

"Anyway," I say, "maybe we should, you know, try to be friends with her or something." He follows my gaze toward Tanya.

"Yikes," he screeches as he realizes what I'm proposing, "you weren't kidding." He takes a deep breath and rationalizes that while we do have six months left in the school year, most of his time will be spent scoping out the local community college in hopes of establishing some serious social ties with college chickie-babes. So, "No, my man, I don't care," is his final answer.

We walk over to Tanya, who looks at us suspiciously as we approach her.

"What do you want?" she asks.

"Tanya, act human," I say.

"Go to hell," she answers.

"No, seriously. I mean, you said it yourself. I'm just like you. You're just like me, and I can vow for Ahmed, he's like us, too." We both look over at Ahmed who pretends to smoke a cigar. "Well, kind of," I say. "Anyway, we thought we'd come over here and talk to you." She looks at us funny, and for the first time I can remember, Tanya doesn't seem to know what to say.

"Just accept it, Tanya, okay?" I tell her. "Move over." I plop down next to her. Ahmed sits down across from us, and she looks back and forth between me and him as Ahmed continues his conversation of the new chickie in ceramics.

"You're such a sexist," Tanya says, unable to resist the urge of telling Ahmed how such labels on women are degrading and disgusting and continue to contribute to the overall inequality of men and women in modern-day society. I side with her, and Ahmed looks like I've just stabbed him in the back but keeps defending his lingo. And pretty soon the bell rings, and we all go our separate ways, but when I ask Tanya if same time, same place tomorrow works for her, she rolls her eyes and says whatever but that she's not eating anything I bring, which I take as a yes.

When I get to drama, Charlotte asks me where I've been and what happened to me as soon as she sees the scrapes on my face. She seems genuinely concerned and worried, and I don't want to lie to her, but I also know I can't tell her the truth right now because it just doesn't feel like the right time or place. So I just shrug my shoulders and tell her not to worry about it.

She looks confused and hurt, and I know she's probably frustrated that I won't say more, especially since things are already weird because of the way we left everything that night. I wish we were alone so I could come clean because even though I might have to resist the urge to kiss her every time I'm near her, I'd rather have her friendship than nothing.

I look over at Charlotte and tell her I just had lunch with Tanya Bate. Her eyes go wide, but she looks happy to have something to talk about, so she asks me to tell her more. I do, letting her know that there was no sinister plan behind it, but that it was actually cool. Then I start rambling about how certain people seem scary to others, which prevents them from really getting to know them or reaching out to them. Then that makes me think of how fear breeds intolerance and insensitivity, which leaves Charlotte with her mouth hanging open and looking at me like I'm a lunatic. But this time I don't care. What is there really to lose?

When we have to shut up because Mrs. C is starting class, I catch Charlotte glancing periodically at me with a funny look on her face and I suddenly realize that to Charlotte VanderKleaton, I am as hard to figure out as she is to me.

• • •

The morning of the exhibit, I wake up with the heaviest feeling in my stomach. I try to shake it off and tell myself it's just nerves, which is mostly true, but I keep looking around, searching for something I don't see.

I'm up before Dad, so the house is silent and still. I sit at our breakfast bar, my thoughts wandering to Mom, while I drink a glass of orange juice. I think I hear echoes in the house, I think they're of Mom and Dad and me. I try to conjure up sounds of us laughing, but it's hard. Did we ever laugh? I feel like I'm in a dream, and actually wonder if maybe I am, if maybe I'm still upstairs in my bed, sleeping. I take the last swig of orange juice and try to block out the ghosts of us. The juice is extra tangy. My senses seem like they're on a hyperacute setting. And then I remember, while we waited at New Day, how I had told Mom about the exhibit tonight.

I don't want to worry because it makes me seem like a traitor, but I do. I worry that she might actually remember, or worse, will decide to show up and surprise me and fuck everything up. I start panicking, even as I rationalize that she's two hours away and she probably doesn't remember. But even if she did remember, I'm sure her program facilitator wouldn't let her come. But if she did come, if she saw those pictures, what would happen?

I get ready for school, the sweet citrus of the orange juice quickly turns into an acidic, bubbling mess that seems to be eating away at my stomach. I belch burning burps the rest of the day, and with every passing hour, minute, and second, I get more and more worried that Mom will show up.

The rest of the day is excruciating and all I can think of is being in bed tonight, when it is all over, when everything that's going to happen just happens and it's done. By the time I get home, it's become my mantra: *Tonight when I'm in bed, it will all be over. Tonight when I'm in bed, it will all be over.* As long as I keep saying it to myself, I can make it through the rest of the night. As a distraction, I start wondering how my first appointment with my therapist will go tomorrow. I wish it were today instead.

When I get home, I take a long hot shower and get ready. When Dad gets home, he does the same, and an hour later we're in the car headed to Rennington. The bits of snow on the side of the road make me think of Mom, so I don't talk much, which Dad interprets as me being nervous because he keeps telling me not to worry, that everything will be fine. But I'm not worried about my collection or winning or losing. I'm worried that Mom will show up. And even though I feel like we're making progress somehow, this stresses me to no end and makes me feel like everything is still the same.

"You got something prepared in case you win, Sport?" He bites his lip when he realizes how he just called me Sport.

"Uh, yeah," I lie.

Dad starts whistling, the way he does when he doesn't know what else to do, and I wonder why things still seem so weird and uncomfortable with him. I wonder if it will get better because I know I didn't used to feel this way all the time. I remember feeling close to him, but I can't remember when that was. I look over at him. He turns to look at me, then back at the road, then back at me.

"What?" he asks.

I want to tell him he looks different to me somehow. I want to tell him that I'm pissed about what he did, and that hating him and Mom and especially some stupid lady I don't even know takes a big toll on me. And I want to tell him how I'm scared Mom will show up tonight. I want to warn him about my photo collection.

I want to tell him that even though I tried not to, I threw up after school today.

"I'm just worried. I hope everything goes okay," I say because it's better than totally lying.

He nods. "It will," he says, and I pray that he's right.

• • •

Mr. Killinger meets all of us in the lobby. The other finalists are there, as well as several other kids from my photography class, and Ahmed.

"Great, you're here," Mr. Killinger says. "Are you ready?"

No, I'm not, but I nod. Ahmed comes up and gives me a big slap on the shoulder. "Let's go, player." I take a deep breath. Mr. Killinger starts telling us that the department head is eager to meet all of us and keeps commenting on what fine photographers we are, blah, blah, blah. He leads us down the hallway and into a big open room that has several paintings on display.

This main room opens into three other rooms. In the center, encased in glass are two sculptures, one very large and the other medium sized. The smaller one is odd. It looks like a bunch of twisted tree limbs roped together with delicate birds perched on top, but then these weird tree hands are attached to the ends of the limbs and they look like they might attack the birds.

The larger sculpture is of a woman sitting, a robe or sheet draped across her from the waist down, but the rest of her is exposed. The detail to her body makes me look away quickly, but not before I notice that her face is practically featureless. I want to go look at it closely, study her face and see if it really is as blank as it looks, but I'm too embarrassed that people will think I just want a cheap thrill or something. Ahmed's eyes open wide, and he chokes out a half laugh/half cough. He looks over at me with a stupid grin on his face, but I pretend not to notice and study the smaller sculpture instead.

The crowd is a strange mix of well-dressed adults and concert T-shirt, jeans, and beanie-wearing college kids. I scan the room. No Mom. I loosen my tie, feeling suddenly uncomfortable in my button-down shirt and khakis. I wish I'd worn jeans. I decide to ditch the tie altogether and shove it in my pocket.

An old, bald man comes up to Mr. Killinger. I am so intrigued by the twirly white mustache on his face that somehow draws even more attention to his shiny, bare head, that I barely pay any attention to what he is saying. His mustache twitches and moves with every word he says, and it looks exactly like the kind you see on cartoons. It loops upward and curls perfectly on both sides, giving him the strange appearance of having an unusually gleeful grin.

"Ah, Luka, these must be your prized students," he says and his mustache twitches. He smiles, I think, as he looks at us.

"Yes, indeed," Mr. Killinger says proudly. He introduces all of us to Dr. Hoyt, the head of the Fine Arts department, professor, and his mentor.

We shake hands with the man, who continues looking at us. He reminds me of the Monopoly guy. Then I think of how Mom used to play Monopoly with me sometimes.

Mr. Killinger walks us over to one of the three smaller rooms, where each of the three walls holds one of the collections from our class. My collection is on the far wall, directly opposite of the arched entrance we'd just come through.

"There they are," Mr. Killinger says, holding out his arm as we all walk into the room. Steve-O and Lisa walk to their collections with their different groups of friends and family.

I stand still. I suddenly get the urge to turn around and run. I can't believe I did this; people are not going to understand why I did what I did. Dad . . . God, Dad would hate me forever, and if Mom showed up, this would just set her off. What the hell was I thinking? Not to mention Charlotte who would never speak to me again once she realized I didn't use the pictures of her.

"Come on, my man," Ahmed says as Dad comes up behind us. They start walking toward the photographs, but I stay where I am. I don't think I can move.

I stare at them from here because each image is already etched in my memory. I don't have to get any closer. I watch Dad and Ahmed as they make their way over to my exhibit.

Instead of having the story progress with each picture, I wanted the viewer to get the whole story at once, so I arranged my frames for that effect. I see Dad slow down as he processes the images. I can't see his face, only the back of his head. I watch him run a hand through his hair. What's he thinking? What if he doesn't understand? I keep my eye on his back. His shoulders slouch. I had justified these pictures to myself so many times, but now

I really think I made a huge mistake. Ahmed looks back at me with a look that lets me know he gets it.

The photos are black and white. The first picture is of Dad blindfolded, and the last one is of me blind-folded. They remind me of hostage pictures, which I guess in some ways I felt like they were. Dad had lip-stick on his otherwise crisp, white shirt, and even though you can't see his eyes, you can tell how he's feeling.

I made sure the distance of my picture with the blindfold was the same as Dad's, so the dimensions of the picture would be the same if they were lined up next to each other. I look at the one of myself, in that chocolate smeared T-shirt and my stuffed mouth. It's still really hard for me to look at it.

In between my picture and Dad's, there are five pic-tures of Mom. I struggled trying to find a way to show she was gone, but that she was still there—always there. I had some photos of her stored in my camera, so even though I hadn't been able to photograph her, I was able to use this close-up I had taken of her when I first got my camera. I cropped bits of her; her mouth, her fore-head and hair, her eye and eyebrow, and her cheek, and I used them individually, so there were four pictures that were little pieces of Mom. And in the very center, there's the full picture of her intact, but I blurred and manipulated the image so you can't see her well, so it looks like she moved at the last second. The message of her photographs is that you never get the full picture of who she truly is, not even those closest to her.

I played around with the shading of each, so while

you can definitely make out each photograph, they still have a dark, foreboding look. Perhaps even then, I knew something bad was going to happen.

I turn my focus back onto Dad. He shakes his head now. What had I expected?

He finally turns back and looks at me. It's not the expression I had expected to see on his face. In that one look he gives me, I can tell all the things he wants to say but can't, and has never been able to say. I realize how alike we are, how we can't say the things we want to say. And I suddenly feel this surge of sympathy for Dad. I know he sees things in those pictures he had previously chosen to not see, had ignored, and had purposely missed, because I had too.

"Hey, you." I hear a voice from behind me. I turn around and it's Charlotte. She's here.

"You're here," I say. And she looks so good that my heart feels as crushed as the night I lay in the falling snow on her front lawn. Her hair is pulled back, and she looks all soft and gauzy in the white sweater she's wearing that I just want to lay my head on her chest and see if she feels like a cloud. I have to stop. I can't keep falling for this girl.

She gazes over my shoulders and sees the photos behind me.

"Where's your . . . is that it?" she asks, walking past me. And I wish I had explained to her why she's not up there, but now it's too late. She looks back at me, and I don't know if that's shock or betrayal or confusion on her face, but it unnerves me. I look back at Dad who is still standing in front of and staring at the images, and

I suddenly feel like I've done the worst thing possible to both of them. How I have set them both up in a way. I look at all the people in the gallery, the strangers I'm sharing my darkest secrets with and realize what an idiot I am. I need to get out of here.

I start heading out of the room just as Dr. Hoyt comes in, adjusting some kind of small microphone attached to the lapel of his jacket.

"Can I have everyone's attention, please?" he says as his voice comes through hidden speakers. I need to get away from here. But Mr. Killinger spots me making a getaway, and he makes his way across the room and follows me.

"Charlie? Hey, Charlie!" I walk faster, but he catches up with me right outside the main gallery room, and he grabs me by the elbow. The hall is now empty as everyone makes their way to the room with the photo collections. The speakers are in every room, including the hallway, so we hear Dr. Hoyt's voice everywhere. Most people are making their way toward the photo exhibits.

"What are you doing?" Mr. Killinger asks. "He's about to announce the winner of the scholarship."

"I know," I say. "I . . . I just can't go through with it. I'm not going to win anyway, but I can't be in there."

"Charlie, you deserve to be in there," he says.

"No, it's not that, it's just, those pictures, my pictures, I . . ."

His face softens. "Charlie, I know it's easier to hide behind the lens, trust me. I know you feel vulnerable, exposed, but, man, what you did. That's amazing. That's the kind of rawness only a true artist can capture."

"But . . ."

"No, listen to me . . . putting yourself out there, that's the kind of thing that's going to make things better. Being honest and reaching out like that, Charlie, that's what you have to do." And the way he says it makes me believe him.

Dr. Hoyt's voice is still booming over us, explaining the contest and the difficulty of choosing just one winner, but that the photographer they had chosen displayed a rare honesty in his collection that was apparent from first glance.

"Ladies and gentlemen, I am proud to announce the winner of our first novice photography contest and the first recipient of the Robert Koster Young Photographer scholarship. And the winner is . . ." Killinger keeps his gaze on me and doesn't let go of my elbow.

"Mr. Charlie Grisner and his collection, entitled *Us*." Applause follows his announcement.

I look at Mr. Killinger, sure I didn't hear right. He smiles and says, "You did it Charlie. Did you hear that? It's you." I shake my head because this can't be real. He nods. "That applause? That's for you, Charlie. Now get in there. Go." I don't move. "Go!" he yells.

My brain isn't functioning, and I just do what he says. I run down the hall, through the main gallery, and into the room where Dr. Hoyt is speaking, and the applause is slowly dying down as people start looking around confused.

"Mr. Charles Grisner," Dr. Hoyt repeats, right before

he spots me making my way to my collection. "Ah, there you are. And now perhaps Mr. Grisner will say a few words."

Even though Mr. Killinger had told me to be prepared to make a speech in case I won, I hadn't thought I would really win and after everything with Mom, I never came up with a speech. And now, here I was, in front of all these people, out of breath from running here and from the disbelief of actually winning, with nothing to say. But I know I have to go up there and talk. I find Dad in the crowd, and he's applauding like crazy. My feet keep moving and I feel like I'm not even really me as I head toward the small lectern that has suddenly been placed next to my collection. I take a deep breath and step up on the podium.

I clear my throat and start, "Um, hi, and thanks. Thank you, Dr. Hoyt and Rennington College for this opportunity." I take a deep breath because I really feel like I'm going to fall over. "So, um, yeah, my name is Charlie Grisner." Am I talking? Are these words really coming out of my mouth? "And this is my collection. The inspiration for it is my mom." My voice starts quivering as soon as I mention her. I don't know if I can go through with this, but then I just start thinking of Mom and Dad and me and everything that's happened, what's happening right now, and what might happen in the future. And I just keep talking.

"See, my mom. She's not like other people." My voice refuses to recover; it shakes and trembles. "She leaves. She's left a lot throughout my life. I've never known where she goes, I don't know why she goes, but she does, and she leaves us behind. And it's hard on me and my dad and I . . . we've never known what to do about it so . . ." I don't look at him because if I do, my voice will stop working all together. "We just go on, but that was a mistake because, because we almost, she almost . . ." But I can't say it, I can't say she almost died because . . . I can't. "And it made me realize how much I love her, and it made me want to understand her and stop blaming her and hating her for leaving."

The room is silent and I can feel the swell of emotion in my chest rising to my throat. I clear my throat, look down, and will the stinging in my eyes to go away. I have to do this. I have to say this.

"I thought that maybe these pictures might help me figure her out, figure us out, my dad, me, my family. That maybe I could see in them what I can't see when life is going on all around us. Maybe in the frame of a picture, I might be able to zoom in and piece things together, because . . ." I stop and take another deep breath. "Because, I need to know who she is, who we are. I don't want to pretend everything's okay anymore. I just want to know who she is."

More words start coming out of my mouth, and the more I talk, the more I realize that I had been afraid of Mom in some ways and how even though she's the one who left, we're the ones who stayed clear of her. I think of Tanya Bate and how people won't go near her. I wonder what we're all afraid of, because in the end, we're all the same. Even those who are different. All we have to do is come out of the boxes we build around ourselves because the truth is we're the ones who close ourselves up, hide ourselves in our own tiny compartments, leaving no room for anyone else. And if we come out and learn to trust people and actually care to know one another, then maybe we would understand each other better. I keep going on and on, and even though I think I'm not making sense anymore, I can't stop talking, even as I look over everyone's heads and the arch above them.

I scan the audience, which is the worst thing I can do because Dad is crying, which makes me start to choke up and then I see Mr. Killinger who is nodding and cheering me on. And there's Ahmed, the way he's always been, weird and spazzy and cool and the greatest friend in the world. He pounds his fist over his heart and throws me a peace sign.

And next to him is Charlotte, whose eyes are glistening and who I don't understand and maybe never will. She's looking back like she's seeing me for the first time, and there's something about the way she does it that gives me hope that maybe now she'll let me get to know her, too, the real her. And I know that as soon as I'm done with this damn speech, as soon as the two of us can be alone, I'm going to tell her everything. And also, how she doesn't have to live up to some unrealistic idea of who I perceive her to be because if anyone knows that nobody's perfect, it's me. And I won't ask her to save me because I know she can't, the same way Dad couldn't save Mom. I just want to know who she really is, and I want her to know who I really am.

Then it starts—an applause so loud and crazy that I think the earth might shatter and swallow me whole.

And it's over; I'm done and I'm not even sure what I said, but I know it was right because I feel like the world's been lifted off my chest, where I've been carrying it all this time. I look around, notice people looking at me; but not like they feel sorry for me, not like they pity me. I think they understand me. I want to remember this—the applause, the looks on their faces, how good it feels to say what I had to say. I look over at the pictures of Mom on the wall, and it's bittersweet. She's here, but not here.

I look out at the audience again. And that's when I see her, standing by herself in the main room right outside of this one. She's framed by the arch that separates the two rooms. And it's like I dreamed her up because she's smiling and she's clapping and tears are falling down her face, like she's proud of me. I can't remember when I felt so full. And I don't try to figure out if she hatched some elaborate escape from New Day Center, or if she convinced one of the counselors to bring her here on a day pass, or if she'll still be here if I blink. I don't know because I don't know Mom. But I'm glad she's here now. Maybe, just maybe, the laws of the universe will work in my favor this one time. I think of all the crap I've been dealt and wonder if this is the beginning of something new. Maybe things will be okay this time. Maybe I'll finally learn who Mom is. Maybe we'll be all right for once.

I close my eyes and see all the puzzle pieces floating around in my mind. I hear them and watch them click in place—and that's when they finally become clearer to me. I see how nobody can save any one person, but also, how everybody needs someone. I see how shutting your-self up in a tiny compartment can suffocate you. I see how bottling everything up and stuffing it down can weigh you down. I see how sometimes you need complete darkness to see things you couldn't or didn't want to see before. I realize that sometimes what's real isn't pretty, but what's pretty isn't always real. And now I see that I can be the real Charlie Grisner.

I take a deep breath, open my eyes, and breathe.

ACKNOWLEDGMENTS

My eternal gratitude to my family:

My husband, Fernando: Because I never knew such goodness before you—everything good can be traced back to the day I met you.

My children, Ava and Mateo: Because you inspire me to be better. Because you teach me lessons nobody else can. Because your sweetness cuts right to the heart of me.

My brother, David: Because in your quietness, I've always sensed a kindred spirit.

My parents, David and Miriam Torres: Porque ustedes han vivido el sueño Americano y saben que estas calles no son hechas de oro, pero de lagrimas y gran sacrificio. Como los quiero y admiro. De sus lagrimas, flores.

Also, my sincerest thanks and appreciation to those who guided me on the road to publication, particularly:

My friend Margarete Bermudez: Because you read the really early, terrible drafts of this and you're still my friend.

My agent, Kerry Sparks: Because you saw something in this and believed in it. Thanks to you, Charlie found a home and I realized a dream.

My editor, Marlo Scrimizzi: Because your incredible talents truly completed this book and made it the work it is today.

Ryan Hayes: For the amazing cover and interior design that just so perfectly fits Charlie's story.

And the team at Running Press for helping make this book a reality.

JENNY TORRES SANCHEZ studied English at the University of Central Florida and taught high school for several years. *The Downside of Being Charlie* is her debut novel. Sanchez also writes short stories, many of which are rooted in her Hispanic culture. She currently lives in Florida with her husband and children. Visit her online at **jennytorressanchez.com**